Samantha's Perseverance

Gail Mazourek

Lodi Whittier Library
PO Box 208
2155 E. Seneca Street
Lodi, NY 14860

Gail Mazourek, Author of *Samantha's Anguish*, skillfully and sensitively involves teens and adults alike in learning about slavery and the rights of women in 1782. As the novel closed, I didn't want it to end, but book three awaits!

Julia Bentley Macdonald, Cornell University graduate, Child Development and Family Studies. NYS

~~*~~

(*Samantha's Anguish*) I thoroughly enjoyed this story. This one was even better than the first one of the series, which was well done. It was hard to put down once I started reading. There is so much information concerning what life was like at that time. I'm definitely looking forward to the third book in the series.

Bonnie Covington, New York State

~~*~~

Samantha's Anguish is the second book of a series based on the life and times of some of Gail's own family members during the American Revolution. Join Samantha as she spends time at Mount Vernon with the very first First Lady, Martha Washington. The adventure keeps growing from there.

Diana Pierce, Pennsylvania

Found in the back of the book:

1 --Chapter notes:

They explain some terms for a few of the chapter words. They are interesting reads and clarify the 1780 (s) era.

2 -- Bibliography

3 -- About the Author

4 -- Patriot Recognition

~~*~~

Other books by Gail Mazourek

(See them on www.amazon.com and Kindle, also http://www.gailmart.com, Goodreads, and Twitter.)

Samantha's Revolution – a novella
Samantha's Anguish – book two, a novel

Samantha's Perseverance
Book three, a novel

by Gail Mazourek

Tharsa G Creations

Samantha's Perseverance Copyright ©
2014 by Gail Mazourek

ISBN: 978-0-9904156-2-6 (paperback)
ISBN: 978-0-9904156-3-3 (eBook)

Library of Congress: LCCN 2014918936
Tharsa G Creations, Box 213, Newfield, NY

Author: Gail Mazourek
Cover Art: Gail Mazourek

Editor: Largely looked over and advised by
Cynthia Machamer

Author Photo: by Roblyn Potter

Printed in the United States of America

10 9 8 7 6 5 4 3 2 1   first edition

DEDICATION

In memory of Mother, Lora Babbette (Crippen) Voorheis. I am one of her eight children, from the middle of our family group. All were loved, each as an individual. She guided each of us in her unique way. Thank you, Mom. *Gail Mazourek*

Samantha's Perseverance

Contents

Chapter **1**

Widow's Testimony
May 1783

Sixteen-year-old slave, Cretia, murdered the village doctor and confessed when she turned herself in with the weapon. But then she closed her mouth shut and refused to give an answer for why she did it. The sheriff demanded that she speak-up but she remained mute behind bars in his jail. The people in Yorkville and the surrounding hamlets and villages were dissatisfied and intent upon their demand for an answer as they waited for the trial. The village had bustled with people from neighboring townships and colonies for the whole week before the slave faced examination by law.

Samantha stayed a prisoner inside her own home while she looked out at the busy village several times a day. The observance of the actions of some of these people compelled Samantha to equate them with snakes in the grass. She believed they slithered and slipped into cracks of her and Cretia's lives to strike wherever they could to undermine truths, thoughts and power. On a quest for news for these people, reporters pried, spied, and intruded for the sake of furtive snooping.

Lawyer, Isaac Hogan kept her informed of his preparations to insure that she, an injured party, and Cretia the slave would be able to tell their story in court. She trusted his council and welcomed his sense of justice for slaves, which was not shared by many.

It was not usual for a woman or a slave to be allowed to speak in court. If they kept their silence now, the court would have no recourse but to hear them at the only time they had agreed to talk.

Isaac sometimes twisted the ends of his handle-bar mustache, the only facial hair he allowed on his otherwise clean shaven face. He inspired confidence in himself from others due to his immaculate appearance in a brass-buttoned suit with his stylish ruffled shirt that peeked from beneath the lapels and cuffs. His dark hair was as neat as his attire, pulled back straight and caught with a thin black tie. His hairstyle reminded Samantha of her brother, seventeen-year-old Jonathan. She smiled at the fond memory brought to mind of her oldest brother, whom she longed to see again.

Rumors abounded that the black population harbored hatred and they were suspected to be on the verge of mischief or worse against their white owners. Harsh treatment of slaves by masters along with their possible guilt caused fear to run high. They worried about blacks poised in secret to harm their owners.

Samantha Crow Goodson, the youngest widow, known in the village, at 15 years old, heard those stories from her inherited slaves, Auntie Geneva, Uncle Percy and their son, Leroy. She had full confidence from the trio, trust that she had earned through past association. They were her constant source of information along with her lawyer, Isaac Hogan. Each of them walked about, without extra notice, in the width of the dirt roadway and on wooden boardwalks that lined the fronts of buildings on either side of the dusty strip.

If Samantha dared to venture outside her own front door, her notoriety among the population qualified as entertainment. Citizens near and far waited for a glimpse of her. The attention stemmed from her status as a young bride of nearly two-days and as the recent widow, of the murdered Doctor Goodson.

Samantha did not speak about the death and her solid pact with Cretia gave them both absolute intentions to refuse to talk until their appearances in court at Cretia's trial. She and the ill girl in the jail intended to present the story in a united front when circuit court convened. Until then, another week away, Samantha continued to endure groups of people, men, women, and children, in front of her house. Arms extended to point out that the young former wife lived there. They hung about all hours of the day in hope that she would appear. If a reporter had convinced her to tell, he would be favored. She would not come out until the sheriff and his deputy came to escort her safely to visit Cretia in the jail and to the court on the day of the trial.

A tent city sprung up as the need for goods and services became immediate. The blacksmith had so much work that he hired a Wheelwright, a young farmer, who repaired everything including the many wagons, the wheels, and harness rigs for horses. Other farmers boarded horses in their pastures at high cost. Only a couple of fields further out from the village center came at a decent price.

The saloon enterprise that never closed thrived and provided a constant disruption of unruly patrons, some who could not hold their liquor well. Fights and brawls were commonplace in the dirt expanse down the main thoroughfare of the village.

The local all-time citizens viewed it as a rare chance to make extra money. They would put-up with the noise at all hours until the conclusion of the trial, which promised to bring all of it to an end. Many of the seedy, brawling newcomers used it as an excuse to sew wild oats while away from their regular lives that had temporarily been left behind, or had been escaped from.

A tent full of women with enlivened reputations of ill repute were in the thick of the action raking in money. Their seductive canopy, located behind the bar that never closed, kept the same pace. The saloon owner charged the madams for the prime location. A group of church ladies staged an objection but were driven out by the booing of drunken patrons who spilled out from the entrance. The newspapers covered it on their back pages in small paragraphs.

Merchants appeared within the sudden growth of people since money could be made. Many homes became boarding houses and rented one or two rooms out at high prices.

Lawyer Isaac Hogan had a room over his office, which went for that same purpose. He remarked to his widowed friend, Samantha Goodson that he needed the income to care for his family. He was proud to have his new baby son born healthy with Samantha Goodson's midwife help over two weeks earlier. His wife, Catherine, and two children were doing well and Samantha had been able to stop the once-a-day visits to the Crow-Hogan farm after initial fulfillment of her bargain. She had bartered her midwifery and follow-up care to pay the lawyer for representation of Cretia at trial. Samantha became good friends with Catherine Hogan. The same farm had been Samantha's home until her parents moved north.

Percy, who was Cretia's uncle and also Samantha's inherited slave, had a garden at the Hogan farm prospering with no allowance for weeds. He knew that her grandmother had been responsible for the profusion of rose bushes with thyme growing underneath. A few days before the trial opened, Percy said, "Miss

S'manthy, it would be a shame to leave all of your roses behind since they were planted by your grandmother. Would you like me to take cuttings and propagate roses for Goodson House?"

Her answer was immediate. "What a lovely idea, Uncle Percy. I will want rose cuttings to take with me when I move to Ohio Country to be near my family. I will auction off the house and furnishings that I cannot take with me. Rose cuttings will require Isaac's agreement to allow the removal of some of them since he lives on the grounds. None will be planted at Goodson House. Can you do it on that basis for me, so they can survive travel?" she asked.

"Yes, Miss S'manthy. I will start them early so they will travel in good health on a wagon. Are you able to say how long before you leave here?" he said.

"Leaving a pace takes planning and work, Uncle Percy, and I need to talk this whole thing over with you and Auntie Geneva after the trial. It needs to be put in logical steps, and when the time comes, get started on them," she said. "The time cannot be determined yet since there is so much to think about. I make myself tired with thinking too much about it. I need to let it go until after the trial. The important thing now is preparation for Cretia's trial and making sure her reasons for why she killed Dr. Goodson become known," Samantha said.

"I can wait to talk to you about it, Miss S'manthy," Percy said. "The trial takes most all of mine and Geneva's thoughts, too. We felt like the tension over Cretia could use some relief with a good idea spoken of. It is news to us that you are considering moving from here and will take roses away with you."

~~*~~

The sheriff made it clear that more deputies would be on hand for the trial because opinions ran high. He wanted the trial handled according to lawful procedure with no damage to his reputation. Isaac Hogan mentioned to Samantha that he thought the sheriff had his eyes on a run for higher office.

"It is no matter to me since I will be leaving these parts. It will keep him honest on matters between opposing sides, so that he does not have bad publicity in the newspaper," Isaac said. "In ordinary times he would be more relaxed, but with the atmosphere thick with reporters, he would not get away with much. They are looking for any spikes of news available while they wait on the trial and will jump at the chance if he makes any mistake."

"I agree that it will keep him honest as sheriff but what about the surprise news you just spoke of? When will you leave these parts?" Samantha asked.

"It is possible that we will leave as soon as we can harvest the garden and take food with us to make sure we are successful. There is also the business of wrapping up your legal affairs. It means we may go in about three months but no later than the end of August. Our dilemma is that we don't know our destination yet," Isaac said.

Samantha's mind raced ahead while Isaac spoke. "My destination, which could be arranged around the same time frame as your move, is Ohio Country. Maybe it will coincide for our households to go together and help each other in the process. Why are you leaving?" Samantha asked.

"I already wore out my welcome in these parts with folks who do not believe in freedom for slaves. I took on several jobs to make legal documents for emancipation and I have many more I'm obligated to finish before I stop. Slave owners say it makes trouble for them when emancipated slaves talk to their slaves whom they have no intention to set free. There's talk among lawyers and statesmen that the state of Virginia may enact a law that forces freed slaves to leave the state within one year of gaining freedom. I believe such a law will eventually be on the books. I already worry about my family alone at the farmstead because Catherine is an easier target than I am here in the middle of the village. My reputation will be made worse when I gain more notice in the newspaper over Cretia's trial. That, Widow Goodson, is good reason to move on. I will talk to Catherine about Ohio Country," Isaac said.

Samantha couldn't stop smiling as she listened to him talk. "I believe we should move you into Goodson House as soon as you think Catherine will feel safer here with the children. I hope you are serious about the location of Ohio Country. My folks will be helpful people to settle near," she said.

Now it was Isaac who could not erase a smile from his face. "Widow Goodson would be a fine neighbor, too," he said. "We will have to get serious about plans after the trial but right now it is all we should be thinking of."

"Please consider a move for Catherine and the children into my home even before the trial is over. Perhaps you can give her a chance now to think about it so she can decide if it would be safer for herself and the children," Samantha said.

"Thank you for the generous offer. I will let her know about the possibility of it, but she enjoys watching the garden grow and would find it hard to leave," Isaac said.

~~*~~

Samantha had been escorted by two deputies while she and Auntie Geneva had both gone to the jail to visit Cretia the day before the trial. They each wanted to assure her they cared and Cretia had no doubt of that. She held in her mind that she had very little life left and wondered if she might actually die of consumption before they could convict her and carry out the sentence.

Two lawmen were required to escort Samantha back to her door. She closed the heavily hinged, varnished walnut behind her, glad to escape from prying eyes. She knew Isaac had been right about the need for her security.

Nothing had changed for Cretia. She was going to die of consumption or hanging, one or the other, she believed. She had known that when she killed the evil Dr. Goodson. Her constant worry was whether or not she could tell the story in court. Her worsened cough made it difficult to speak and the court would not be patient nor kind like Miss S'manthy and Auntie Geneva. She wanted a chance to tell the village that the doctor was wicked and had deserved the same in return. If she, as a slave, told it before the trial, she would not be allowed to speak about it in court. She was being forced to talk in court, but her tactic of silence was the force getting her the audience. Her chance was in front of her today.

The circuit court judge pounded the gavel to bring the court to order and the packed room quieted down. Judge Hiram Hobbs warned the spectators that any interference or undue noise would result in contempt of court with substantial charges following. Cretia never stopped her coughing, but a contempt charge did not apply to her because she could not stop and could not pay. Judge Hobbs was in control of his courtroom and gave one chance for people to leave if they desired before the start. He announced, "If there be anyone not wishing to stay here until mid-morning recess, go now as this court will not tolerate interruption." No one left and it was quiet except for Cretia's coughing.

Widow Goodson sat near lawyer Isaac Hogan to be sure she heard every word and could refute anything brought up by the prosecution that she thought or knew to be untrue. She listened to both lawyer's openings as each stated their case. She found it focused and intriguing but not hopeful for Cretia. The facts could not be disputed. Both lawyers believed Cretia had killed Dr. Goodson, but the point of view of each agent was holding the crowded room in its spell. The opposing lawyer made it clear that he was shocked that a woman and her slave should be allowed in a court of law to testify. "It can lead only to tainting a domain meant exclusively for men," his voice boomed.

Samantha was appalled that many were staring at her to excess as she used her fan in the hot courtroom. She wondered if she would fall asleep in the stifling heat of people's body odor and high temperature as the day ensued. She counted on the fan reviving her. How could Cretia remain sitting upright? Yet she did while she coughed and listened to the lawyers presenting each side.

The first break was welcome and people rushed about, some hurrying to privies behind buildings and some to water wells where they pumped fresh liquid to relieve their thirst. They had only half an hour and Samantha took advantage of it only to walk around the courtroom. She would need an escort if she walked to her house and she did not want to cause that distraction. Auntie Geneva and Uncle Percy also stayed in the courtroom.

"Miss S'manthy, we are worried about the cruel agony it causes for Cretia to sit up too long," Auntie said.

"I'll speak with Mr. Hogan and try to get a bed for her," Samantha said. She spoke with him as soon as he came back in and he agreed to ask for the mercy of the court.

The magistrate spoke with both lawyers in front of his bench and decided there would be no bed, which could cause pity for the defendant. He banged the gavel to announce his ruling and promptly continued.

The legal referee was forced to change his opinion when Cretia fell over within the next half hour. She slipped down silently and was unable to get up. She was only able to cough. Auntie made no sound with her crying. Samantha was in danger of contempt of court at any moment. She remembered that Isaac had cautioned her against showing her opinion over judicial decisions she did not agree with.

Her thoughts could not be stopped. *How can Cretia live through this inhumane treatment? How can these people stand to watch it?*

The cot was brought. Auntie and Percy silently picked Cretia up and placed her on it. They were not held in contempt for the necessity of moving about. Samantha watched the frail form of her friend as she lay there in the blue dress that had been Samantha's own. It was the best dress Cretia had ever worn and it would serve only for a court trial, dying and burial. Samantha's tears were silent and wet, hid by her fan as she dabbed her eyes with an embroidered handkerchief. She believed Cretia slept off and on until noon with intermittent coughing.

It was after the midday dinner break when both lawyers finished presentations of their views with protests of opposing information that questioning of Cretia was to start. All witnesses and one defendant were sworn in again. They stood where they were, Samantha, Geneva, and Percy with three others. They were Pastor Bailey and the two other witnesses to the marriage of Dr. Goodson and Samantha Crow. Pastor Baily had also performed the marriage. They were all able-bodied, but Cretia could only sit halfway up just long enough to raise her right hand over her heart.

Isaac Hogan was gentle with his very ill client, but the prosecutor was not on her side and disliked what he perceived as sympathy for her exaggeration of illness. His belligerence showed in his questioning of her and he became angry when she remained lying on the cot. He tried to have her held in contempt and the courtroom erupted into laughter. The gavel sounded and the laughter stopped dead.

"If another outburst occurs, this courtroom will be free of spectators for the remainder of the day," Judge Hobbs declared.

Cretia was able to answer yes or no, but the prosecutor wanted explanation of why she had committed the stabbing. "It would help this court to know, before sentencing, why you did it," he said to Cretia. "Now explain to the court why you stabbed Dr. Goodson until he died." The silent courtroom full of people seemed not to be breathing while they waited for Cretia's answer.

"I was beaten and raped," she coughed, "and my arm was broken by the devil doctor," cough... "Miss S'manthy," coughing..., "was beaten and raped," Cretia coughed. It had remained silent in the courtroom as everyone waited for her to get her words out.

"Who is Miss S'manthy?" the impatient prosecutor demanded.

Cretia sat halfway up and coughed without control. When she gained momentary constraint, she turned slightly and pointed to Widow Goodson before collapsing back onto the cot to cough again. Samantha was fanning her warm face and half hiding behind the moving pleats of her ribbon and rosebud fan.

The judge called for the cot to be moved to the side and directed Widow Goodson to take the stand. Samantha walked slowly to the seat and sat down facing the lawyers.

"The court is sorry for your loss, Mrs. Goodson," the prosecutor stated, as his polite way to start. "Are you known as Miss S'manthy?" he asked.

"Yes, I am known as Miss S'manthy?" she said.

"The defendant is speaking of you who was a married woman at the time and could not be raped since a husband has unconditional rights of access," he said. "Please tell the court your version." His manner of making his statement seemed to assume that the widow's account would oppose her slave.

"I was beaten and raped by Dr. Goodson when I was unmarried, but was working for him. I became pregnant. His violence made me afraid to tell..." The prosecutor stopped her words. "I ask the court not to hear discourse against the spouse since a wife cannot testify against her husband," he said.

The judge spoke decisively. "This testimony will be heard. The complete statement from Widow Goodson is appreciated since she is no longer Dr. Goodson's wife and is testifying on her own account to convey the reason why she believes the death may have come about."

Samantha was glad to start again. "My parents trusted Dr. Goodson just as most people in this community did. He had an evil side he kept hidden, but Cretia and I knew of it firsthand in the worst possible way. Dr. Goodson violated Cretia first by a brutal beating, which I witnessed when he broke her arm. At a later date, he raped her. I was forced to marry Dr. Goodson when he brought Pastor Bailey to the waiting room and took us by surprise to force the marriage and have a certificate of marriage finalized by his witnesses. He did it because he wanted control over me with his child." Samantha took a breath and hurried on with her testimony.

"Dr. Goodson had blamed his wife for not bearing a child and she often wore bruises where he beat her, too. Cretia and I took care of her because the doctor would not go near her and take a chance on contracting her illness. When he beat me in the act of trying to rape me after I was his wife I miscarried my baby. Cretia stopped him when he hit my stomach instead of my face with his fist. Cretia is right that he was a devil doctor, a very evil one," Samantha said. She let out a long sigh and fanned her steaming face.

Several times during Samantha's credible testimony, the spectators in the courtroom gave a barely audible sound of disbelief on hearing of the actions of the deceased doctor, as told by Samantha. It was not their disbelief, but that it was rather incredulous that the evil had not been undetected by most of them. The judge let the subdued noises go as long as they did not over-power the testimony.

The prosecutor's face turned red. "Such a statement from the good doctor's wife is a travesty," he said.

Samantha burst into tears and began shaking. She became too emotional to continue and was reluctantly allowed to step down. Cretia's coughing turned into sobs. Samantha wanted to run to her to console her, but she could not.

Geneva and Percy gave a brief testimony to the court without the prosecutor being allowed to stop them altogether from talking. He put in a request to call Pastor Bailey up as his presence had been required. Pastor Bailey and two witnesses denied knowing that Samantha Crow was forced to marry Dr. Goodson.

Isaac Hogan introduced the marriage certificate, which was signed by Pastor Bailey. Lawyer Hogan was satisfied that all parties had told Cretia's story well while it had been thoroughly validated by Samantha. He was able to let it rest without asking further testimony. The six-man jury found Cretia guilty within the half hour. The trial and verdict were over at the end of the first day. Judge Hobbs scheduled the sentencing for the next morning at 9:00 and court was adjourned.

Cretia was carried back to the jail on the cot, which was the same way she arrived there from her cell.

Reporters rushed out to tell the news and others departed on horseback to relay the day's final report back to their newspaper offices, at great distances in some cases. The second writer in a team stayed so that a reporter was in place for the conclusion and sentencing of the trial for the next courtroom session. Newspapers were clamoring to bark the facts learned, using their colorful descriptions.

The headline the next morning in bold typeface announced: *"Widow Cries Rape Before Marriage."* Samantha read the complete report in the article to Auntie Geneva and Uncle Percy. It reported that: *"Sympathy is as thick as cow's cream in the courtroom for the beautiful Widow Goodson who claims to have been beaten and raped before marriage. Her slave, Cretia, was also beaten and abused."* They reported on the entire episode of how the stabbing death came about and the miscarriage resulted. The account in the *Yorkville Telegraph* said that Isaac Hogan, the slave's lawyer, believed she was morally innocent of the crime. The editorialized version stated: *"How can a black murderess be innocent?"*

Samantha's disgust registered in her voice. "How can they say she was my slave even before marriage? They wrote headlines just to sound sensational and draw a lot of readers and sell papers."

"Miss S'manthy, you told the truth in court and Cretia heard it along with everyone else. You cannot account for what some newspapers report wrong with their arrangement of words," Auntie said.

Chapter 2

Devil Doctor
May 1783

The newspaper headline picked up the theme, Devil Doctor, from the testimony of Widow Goodson and her slave, Cretia. After news that the jury pronounced Cretia guilty, the account told about the Devil Doctor, who previously lived and practiced in their midst. Shock value was played up and ended with the statement that a black murderess would meet her punishment on the gallows on the last day of May.

Samantha was upset that the sympathy was for her and not for Cretia. Cretia had been wronged more than Samantha had and it was not fair that her darker skin should deny her any leniency. "I don't think I can stand it, Auntie, that they will actually hang her," Samantha said.

Auntie reached her hand across the newspaper Samantha had finished reading to her and Uncle Percy. "Miss S'manthy, at least they reported how ill Cretia is and that she collapsed in court. Some folks reading it will have pity for Cretia for all she went through. They heard you tell the truth loud and clear for yourself and Cretia after she could only cough. Word has traveled through all of the black folks communities that you spoke up for Miss Cretia," Auntie Geneva said. "All of our people know you took up for her, Miss S'manthy, and Percy and I know you did, too. It's what counts, Miss S'manthy. She did kill him and that is all they will look at for dealing out punishment." She let go of Samantha's arm and stood up to hug her as they so often did in support of each other over the distress of Cretia's situation and health.

They could only wait for the dreaded last day of Cretia's life. Geneva and Percy's son, Leroy, brought them rumors of bets being waged as to whether she would die of illness first or from hanging. All manner of stories circulated in the saloon and through the village. Percy and Geneva heard them all and reported to Samantha on how people hung on every detail.

Auntie Geneva was the one who brought up the subject of Ohio Country. "Miss S'manthy, me, Percy, and Leroy could help you get to Ohio Country. You can't do it by yourself, moving north to find your folks, and we can't stay around here when we get freedom. We will not be welcome in this village or this state once we are freed. We trust your word and we can wait until arrival in Ohio Country to get legitimate papers of freedom. Percy agrees we should wait and avoid a lot of trouble. We got no trouble to stick with you, Miss S'manthy."

"Auntie! You really want to go, too?" Samantha said. "That's wonderful."

"Yes, Miss S'manthy. Percy talked to me and Leroy about it when he first started the garden out there for Mrs. Hogan. Leroy is old enough at 19 years old to make up his own mind and he wants to go. Percy heard rumors about freed slaves having trouble and not being welcome to stay in Virginia," Auntie said.

"I have heard the very same, Auntie, and it is something I was going to talk to you and Uncle Percy about. Isaac Hogan told me he had inside information. From what he hears, he thinks the law will be passed in the next few years, which will compel freed slaves to leave this state within one year of getting their freedom," Samantha said. "And, that's not all...The Hogan family will possibly be moving to Ohio Country, too. We may have their help and they will have ours to make it easier on all of us. We'll need to wait until they make their decision and see if we all go together."

"Miss S'manthy, more rumors tell about Mr. Hogan losing favor. He is the only lawyer in these parts making out legal papers to free slaves and filing the papers at the county seat," Auntie said.

"It is all true, Auntie, and that is why he may be forced to move to keep his family safe. I have offered to have them move into Goodson House if Catherine feels they should for safety. I will just wait on her decision and leave it at that," Samantha said.

"Those little children will liven up this place, Miss S'manthy," Auntie said.

"They will surely do that," Samantha said with a smile.

"One thing is sure, while we wait for the last day of May, Miss S'manthy. It hangs like a sickness one day at a time for us and Cretia. I believe it will give her some comfort to know we will be leaving for Ohio Country with you later and that you have promised our freedom."

"I want you to tell her, Auntie, and then I will tell her, too, so she has it reinforced from both directions. Your visit tomorrow and mine the next day under deputy escort will be good news for her," Samantha said.

"Maybe we can both attend at the same time on her last day if the sheriff will agree," Auntie said.

"I will ask Isaac how we would be able to convince the sheriff to allow it. The sheriff seems to be hostile toward me over all the work required to keep people away from me while escorting me for visits. He tries to hide it because there is some sentiment on my side in the village. He wouldn't be fair if he could get away without it," Samantha said.

"Time is going fast, Miss S'manthy, way too fast and it grieves me," Auntie said.

"Auntie, it will be hard when the scaffold is built in the street for the hanging. Isaac says we need to steel ourselves for that to happen a day or two before the end of May. It will be done no matter how we feel about it. I don't want to dwell on it," Samantha said. "And another thing, the village will fill with people to over-flowing again. Isaac said to expect unpleasantness and to ignore as much of it as we can."

"We can't stop any of it and no sense beating up our minds about it. You might ask Mr. Isaac when our black folk's preacher can visit Cretia," Auntie said.

"I will ask right away. I know it is important," Samantha said.

~~*~~

May was going fast as they visited Cretia, each on alternating days. Isaac got permission for both Geneva and Samantha to visit on Cretia's next-to-last day and a black clergyman would be her only visitor on her final morning. "The preacher will go as far as the steps of the gallows with her and afterward to the cemetery," Isaac said.

The coughing never stopped and it always made communication slow. Samantha was tired of hearing the sheriff jingle the keys after a few minutes to signal that time was up. She needed more time to talk with Cretia. She no longer hurried out at the start of jingling and the sheriff began leaving the jail when she came in. It was left up to a deputy and it saved face for the sheriff that he could not quite handle Widow Goodson. Samantha liked it that way.

The day before the event, Samantha was with Cretia in her cell when the hammering started on the hangman's platform. Cretia jumped as hard as Samantha did at the startling noise. "What a dreadful sound," she said.

Shock was instant to both of them regardless of expecting it. Cretia started shaking and the coughing was no respecter of fear as it became harsher. Samantha held her until she was calmer. She had nothing she considered more important than to be with her friend.

"I am afraid to die, Miss S'manthy," Cretia confided.

Samantha held her and cried with her. "I know and I would be, too. I possess no power to make anything better or to change anything that has happened," Samantha said. "I only wish I did."

"It is good enough that you are here, Miss S'manthy." After another round of coughing, she said, "Will you be watching..." She could not finish.

"No. I can't. I will stay inside my house. I cannot bear to be there," Samantha said.

"This is the last day ever to see you, Miss S'manthy," Cretia said and repeatedly coughed. "Thank you for my blue dress and for our friendship."

"Our friendship has been a gift to me too, dear Cretia, no reason to thank me," Samantha said.

The sheriff and his jingling keys were back and the pounding to build the hangman's scaffold continued. As Samantha stepped out onto the boardwalk, she wanted to avoid looking at it but it was impossible since the apparatus was in the middle of the street halfway between the jail and her house. The deputy escorting her was in no hurry while he visually inspected the equipment. It was appalling to see several spectators gawking at the weighted sack held up by a rope, which was being used to test the workability of the death platform that had been built. Two young boys were on-lookers and Samantha wondered why anyone would allow them to be there. She used her fan to keep more of the view from her sight and was glad to step inside her own door.

Auntie Geneva was inside, and she embraced Samantha as much for herself as for Samantha. "I am glad our visits are over today, Miss S'manthy. I can't bear to walk past that dreadful sight of the platform like you had to but somehow I will do it to be with Cretia tomorrow," she said. "That mess of people out there, everywhere you turn, sure is a sight." The village had filled with people again just as Isaac said it would.

They sat down together in the parlor and leaned close together in a dejected manner, neither one thinking of supper time approaching. Percy's steps sounded on the boardwalk. Even then they did not get up as he quietly entered and sat down across from them. Auntie Geneva started to move and he tried to discourage her getting up to wait on him.

"You sit still, Geneva. I will find a piece of bread to eat," he said.

She got up anyway. "I need to do what's right and keep going," she said and continued into the kitchen. Samantha followed and together they fixed a sparse meal they had no heart to eat. Percy ate but not with his usual relish of Geneva's comforting food. They had a night to get through and then time would be close for the unthinkable. Samantha and Auntie helped each other cope with the dread of the situation coming closer and no more able to stop it than to stop a stampede of buffalo.

~~*~~

Coffee wafted through to Samantha's senses and she sat up with the morning light streaming into her bedroom. There was no smell of bacon or ham or even biscuits. She knew why. She would have no appetite either. How could she or they or the whole town? She could not understand how some in the town had an appetite for the hanging as if it was entertainment.

Percy and Geneva both told her it was best if she stayed inside and out of sight. They would be there to watch and to claim Cretia's lifeless form. It was the final thing they could do for her.

Samantha's solitary wait dragged on as she dreaded the signal of completion for Cretia's doom. She jumped when she heard the church bells toll their long hollow notes that spoke sorrow to those who loved Cretia. It was final. It was over, the deed done to a poor sick girl. The tolling bells tore at Samantha's emotions, as she fell onto her bed with a scream of anguish. She sobbed into her pillow, "Cretia is dead. Cretia is dead." She sat up and twisted her hands together over her pounding heart. She cried quietly and alone, knowing it was most certainly done as the appointed time had just passed. The silence was just as bad when the donging stopped and an interval of waiting began.

What was the required time before the body could be claimed? Time hung heavy until voices rose in a mournful spiritual, *"Nobody Knows the Trouble I've Seen."* It came from the heartfelt depths of the marchers walking behind and beside the carriage pulled by Samantha's horse, Brown. The seat bore only a still form lying crosswise in a blue dress. Auntie Geneva and Percy were on either side of the buggy as the procession moved up the dirt strip. Samantha walked out onto the boardwalk and into the dirt strip to join them to the end of houses along the road. She would have gone further, but Auntie firmly turned her back in the direction of her house and told her she had come a long way in life with Cretia and it was over. She listened as her tears fell and the spirituals faded into the distance.

Chapter 3

The Lists
June 1783

The morning started quietly and felt empty as soon as Percy and Leroy left the kitchen carrying a dinner with them that Geneva had packed for later. They would eat it at the Crow-Hogan farm where they kept good care of the garden and grounds. Samantha and Auntie had time on their hands and no happy thoughts to fill their minds. Auntie Geneva sighed.

"We can't keep moping around here," she said and threw her dish cloth back to drape over one shoulder. Maybe you can start deciding about your belongings, Miss S'manthy, on what will go with you and what you will auction off. Let us get some work done on that if you want to start, so we don't just sit and wait on full plans to be formed. Waiting.

will drive me crazy and I would rather be busy like Percy. He and Leroy have two garden's, one at the farm and one here to keep them busy," Auntie said.

Samantha was quick to smile and was just as ready as Auntie to get busy deciding what she could do. "I can go to each room and make a written inventory so I know what is here to sell and what I may or may not want to take away with me," Samantha said.

"Maybe we should know first, how many wagons will go and what will fit in them, Miss S'manthy," Auntie Geneva said. "We can't take things we have no room for. Wagons are an important issue and we have to have a driver for each one that is going."

"We have good reason then for a meeting with the Hogans since we do need to know details about the wagons. We can figure it out together if they have decided on going to Ohio Country," Samantha said, "and I am anxious to know their decision."

Auntie and Samantha hugged each other, glad to lift the gloom from their morning. "We will have a long time to grieve in private time, Miss S'manthy. We are better off to keep busy," Auntie said. She stayed in the kitchen to work and Samantha shook her head in agreement before she went to the parlor.

Shortly, Samantha called toward the kitchen. "Auntie," I made a list just for this sitting room and nothing in here is going to Ohio Country."

Auntie appeared in the door of the room. "Miss S'manthy, you sure are happy at the thought of going to your folks in Ohio Country. I believe you and my Percy will get all of us on the road as soon as it can be done."

"You are right, Auntie. I'm going into the exam room where I know I have books and also the black bag filled with tools and necessary things, which have to go with me. I'll make that list now to separate them from items going to auction."

"I best stay in the kitchen if we want supper on time, Miss S'manthy," Auntie Geneva said. She went back into the kitchen humming. She started singing a spiritual and sang as she worked. Samantha hummed along to the comforting voice.

She opened the box with molded velvet forms where knives should be. She thought of the medium size knife, the one used as evidence in Cretia's trial. She wondered how she could get it back from the sheriff and decided to ask Isaac if it was reasonable and possible to have it returned since it had served its purpose for the court. She doubted she would ever have the small knife again and the largest knife, the only one remaining in the box, was the least useful to her. *Where is that small knife?* Samantha wondered.

She fingered the thick medical volumes and knew they must all go with her. With so much knowledge between the pages, she needed to learn something new from them every day. She would not pack them away, not yet while she still had time to read. She picked up the last volume on the end of the shelf next to the black bag. She wanted to place it where she would find it easy to open and read. She thought of Martha Washington with whom she had stayed at Mt. Vernon nearly two years ago. Martha read at night after retiring and Samantha liked that idea because it was a regular way to enjoy learning. Samantha carried the big book to her room and laid it on her bed before she went to the kitchen.

"I think I have to find an auctioneer and set a date for the sale, Auntie. Isaac may know who can do that for us and we can decide when the auction will be held. It has to be near the end of our time here so we can have furniture to use until almost the last day. It's another reason for all of us to talk together about plans," Samantha said.

"Yes, we must plan. I hear Percy and Leroy stepping onto the boardwalk and they are hungry men," Auntie Geneva said. She set food on the kitchen table and stepped to the oven to pull out hot buttermilk biscuits to complement the meal. Percy washed his hands in a waiting basin of water, a daily practice followed by Leroy. They sat down and Percy said the prayer before they began to eat.

Percy soon laid down his biscuit and said, "Geneva, do you know why Widow Goodson is studying me so I can't eat without prying eyes?" He made an effort not to smile.

"Uncle Percy, I adore you and Auntie Geneva like my own folks in Ohio Country where we are all going," Samantha said.

"Girl, you and Geneva been talkin' behind my back?" Percy could no longer hold back his smile. "Now leave a body alone so I don't die of starvation."

Auntie and Samantha were finishing dishes when they heard a knock on the door. They exchanged glances. "I'm not expecting anyone," Samantha said. She went to the door and found Isaac Hogan and his family waiting outside. She said, "Come right in, and welcome."

Catherine's upset was clear.

Isaac spoke up. "Samantha, can we stay here tonight so Catherine feels safe? I'm not sure when she and the children would feel safe enough to go back to the farm."

"Certainly and you are not going back if it is not entirely safe," Samantha said. Her arms circled Catherine. "My home is available as long as you need it, Catherine. We will get beds made up and you will be comfortable here," she said. Catherine burst into sobs.

Auntie Geneva pitched in to help and the three women soon had beds ready for sleeping. The new baby would sleep in a bed made in a bureau drawer pulled out to set on the floor. The little girl, Margaret, would sleep with her parents until she would be at ease in the house and sleep by herself, maybe on a pad on the floor in their room.

"Thank you, Auntie Geneva, for your extra help," Samantha said. "Catherine, before Auntie goes to her cabin, tell us what happened out at the farm, please."

Catherine was still upset, but she told them through her sniffles that earlier a group of men rode down the road to the farm and shot holes in the door frame while she was watching from the garden. "They knew I was right there and did it just to scare me. They shouted some bad words about my husband and said they didn't cotton to a free slaver around these parts playing his lawyer tricks. I was worried about my sleeping children inside. When the men left and I went inside, little Margaret was crying because the shooting woke her. She was more frightened than I was," Catherine said.

"I am so sorry, Catherine, but you and the children will be safe here," Samantha said. She knew Percy had been kept waiting outside for Auntie. "Now you can let Uncle Percy know what went on, Auntie Geneva. You better hurry out there to the boardwalk where he is waiting for you."

"I'll be here a few minutes early in the morning, Miss S'manthy, to fix breakfast for company," Auntie said.

"Thank you, dear Auntie," Samantha said. Geneva hurried out to go with Percy.

"Samantha, I just need to know we are safe and I will help with work here, too. I am thankful for your home being open to us," Catherine said.

"Tonight you rest and we will figure it all out together," Samantha said.

~~*~~

The next evening brought time for discussion. They gathered around the table to talk with Isaac and heard his decision. "I will finish the freedom papers I am working on now but I will not take on any more jobs of this type. It is too dangerous for my family and besides, I have lots of work to square away details for you, Samantha. Some papers are filed but will take time to be concluded after the death certificate is examined at the county seat and accepted," he said.

"We have a lot to talk over, all of us. For now, I just want to ask you to locate an auctioneer. I need to dispose of this house and its furnishings before departure to Ohio Country. Percy, Auntie, and Leroy will be going, too," Samantha said.

"That is good news, Samantha, the more help we all give each other, the easier our trip will be," Isaac said.

"Our trip?" Samantha asked. Her smile was spreading.

"Yes, our trip, Widow Goodson, we have to leave here and Ohio Country is far enough north to be safe for my family. I can set up a law practice anywhere the population is sufficient. I'll find a seller for you, but we need to talk this over with Percy and Geneva, too, about when we can all be ready to leave here. That will determine when we should schedule the auction. We all have plentiful work to do to make it happen. Too many things in your affairs, Samantha, are still hanging out there unsettled and we have to stay to see it through, however long it takes" Isaac said.

"I understand all of that. I'm anxious to get started," Samantha said.

"It is good that you arranged for Percy and Geneva to stay and talk with us after supper this evening," Isaac said. He picked up two-year-old Margaret over his head to hear her squeal with delight. Isaac continued playing with little Margaret. Her delightful laughter was pleasing to the three women while they did up the evening dishes.

Auntie Geneva had made a dessert for all of them to gather around the dining room table so it made the gathering into a happy time. With the table cleared of all food and dishes, the three families started their discussion. Leroy had been invited and his input was needed because he would be working with his father. He was young, muscular, and strong. They counted on him to work hard on anything for his family. He was not one to push himself forward, but took direction from his father.

Isaac let his little girl down gently to play on her own. He was the logical one to start the meeting since he was an organized lawyer used to starting all kinds of proceedings. "The time frame for our move will be determined by finishing legal matters here for Widow Goodson," he said. He looked toward Samantha and wrinkled his nose at her, knowing she was not fond of her status implied by the use of the title. She had been fine with it when it had helped Cretia's case in any small way. "The best guess I have on the completion of such tasks would be late August. The title to this house must be put in your name before selling, which I have been working on," Isaac told Samantha.

"Can we schedule an auction for late August then?" Samantha said.

"Very late August would probably work for us," Isaac said.

"What is the weather like in Ohio Country in the middle of September?" Geneva asked.

Isaac was the one who answered since he had lived in Pennsylvania at one time. "It will be cooler and the ground will be muddy in some places but the trees will still be green with a hint of some starting to turn red, yellow, and orange. The air will have a chill at night by the middle of September when we arrive. We will immediately have to get a place to live and be settled before snow, ice, and freezing settles in for the end of November and December weather. Is anyone here unwilling to go before spring with this new information?" he said. He looked around at each of them, but no one spoke of holding off going.

"Both of the gardens will be harvested by the end of August and we'll have food to take with us on each wagon," Percy said.

"Now that brings up another question. Percy, are you sure of your safety out on the farm to do that work?" Isaac asked.

"Yes Sir. We are safe as long as no freedom papers are filed for me, Leroy or Geneva. It should be kept this way so that we can come and go as we please for the benefit of all," Percy said.

"I am safe with that work, too," Leroy said. Percy nodded toward his son.

"Percy, you will be paid for your work out there when I finish enough of my own paid work to have funds," Isaac said. "You have already used enough labor to assist Samantha to pay me for Cretia's defense."

"We are grateful for the help she had," Percy said.

Samantha was writing on her paper to keep track of their discussion. "I have started an inventory of the house contents, which I am listing for each room. It may be useful for the auctioneer to plan the auction. I also believe each of us should be deciding on the least amount of belongings that each of us can take with us," she said.

"It will help us if we know how many wagons we will have," Isaac said.

"Miss S'manthy has one big wagon for her goods and four strong horses to pull it. One other wagon is smaller and the two mules can pull it," Percy said.

"We also have one big wagon and four horses to pull it," Isaac said.

"Those horses and the wagon should be brought to Miss S'manthy's barn here in the back acre to keep them from being taken from the unoccupied farm. They will be stolen quicker than any vegetable garden," Percy said. They all laughed at his humor.

"Leroy, you could bring them back here tomorrow if Miss S'manthy agrees," Percy said. He looked to her and they all saw her head moving in the affirmative before she spoke.

"Yes, of course, and thank you, Uncle Percy. We do not want to lose them. I believe we should sell the smaller wagon and buy a bigger one. It will require buying another set of mules so we have four to pull a heavier wagon," Samantha said.

"We might swap the smaller wagon for that second set of animals," Percy said. "Leroy, you run across a couple of young mules for sale yesterday, you said?"

"Yes, Sir. I checked the teeth and the legs. The Jacks are big and strong and would be worth swapping the wagon for them. The young'uns are strong-willed and would take a steady hand," Leroy said.

"We could work with the animals, Miss S'manthy, teach them how to behave," Percy said.

"Go ahead and make the swap for us then, as long as you are sure to handle the team in time for late August," Samantha said.

"Well, we agree on three wagons planned, but one of them to be purchased," Isaac said to sum it up. "Three men will keep an eye out for a wagon coming up for sale."

"Your list looks like it is long enough, Samantha?" Catherine said. "Maybe read it back to us?"

"It is a helpful list," Samantha said.

"Number one is a decision to leave at the end of August. Number two, Isaac will schedule an auctioneer for late August. Number three, Uncle Percy and Leroy will continue with gardens and harvesting to be finished at August's end. It is dependent on the preservation of food by Auntie Geneva, Catherine, and me." Samantha said.

"Nice note added about preserving food, Samantha," Catherine said.

"Number four is the swap of the small wagon for the young Jacks, all to be done by Uncle Percy and Leroy, including the training of the team," Samantha continued.

"Number five is finding a bigger wagon, the men seeking a sound one for my purchase. Number six is the ongoing work by Isaac to conclude my legal and financial affairs. Number seven, I will continue written inventory of house contents. The end," Samantha said.

"Not quite the end," Isaac said. "We need the help of a trailblazer to lead the way to Ohio Country. It is not a clear road all the way and we could get lost. A lot of trouble will be saved if we hire someone right from the start."

"Number eight, finding a trailblazer. Can you find a man able to take that job Isaac?" Samantha said.

"Yes I can, and I suggest you and I share the cost by half," Isaac said.

"Agreed," Samantha answered. "Oh, I almost forgot. Can you get my knife back from the sheriff, the one used for evidence at the trial? I have only one blade left in the set for medical practice." .

Percy's head lowered and he pushed both hands back over the hair on his skull, a possible headache.

Isaac said, "We won't be much longer here, Percy." Addressing Samantha, he said, "I will petition in writing for the knife to be returned. Knowing the sheriff, that could take until August, too."

"It doesn't need to be listed, Isaac, but we will bring the horses and wagon from the farm for you tomorrow," Percy said.

They all stood and the men shook hands as equals. Samantha saw that it was a little awkward for Uncle Percy and Leroy since they were not used to being treated equal by Dr. Goodson or the surrounding community in the past. She liked it that Isaac always shook hands with them as he did with all men. She knew they would get used to it and be able to initiate a hand-shake with Isaac themselves in the future. Uncle Percy seemed uneasy, or not feeling so well, but maybe just tired after a long day.

The small family went to their cabin.

Little Margaret was asleep on her father and the baby was nursing in Catherine's arms under a blanket

"I need to have a significant discussion with Samantha and I'll be right in with Margaret," Isaac said. Catharine went to the bedroom with the baby.

Samantha was taken by surprise. "Is something wrong, Isaac?"

"I can't say that I have good news. I have something unsettling to tell you," Isaac said.

Chapter 4

Rumor and Foreboding
June 1783

Samantha's eyes did not leave Isaac's face. "Unsettling? I must hear it," Samantha said.

"There is a rumor that unfortunately I have to pass along without any proof. It comes from a northern source, a man who was near Ohio Country on his way back here to bring another branch of his family north," Isaac said. "He was stopped overnight at a saloon where he camped with his wagon and horses. The talk around the campfire was general, but the man took notice when he heard mention that there were two deaths in lower Ohio Country recently, just after he left there. That would be two weeks ago, I believe."

"Did he give any names?" Samantha asked as she rose from the edge of her seat. Her sense of foreboding was visible to Isaac.

"He heard two names, but not the description of the people involved or how they died. There was a camp disturbance from a drunkard trying to shoot up the place. Consequently, the man who told me of that incident and the deaths was not able to get more information," Isaac said.

"I need to hear those names, please," Samantha said.

"I can see that you are upset, Samantha and I hate to tell you that one name was Crow and the other was Trader," Isaac said.

"Crow...which one?" Her legs weakened and caused her to sit down with a hand over her heart as if to guard against the pain. "Why don't they ever write and let me know how everyone is? Why?" Samantha said.

"We don't have enough information about this or their reasons either. I'm sorry, Samantha. I know you have expressed a lot of love for your family and it seems certain they return your love. Shouldn't you just wait and see what happens and keep right on loving them?" Isaac said.

"I know they love me. I didn't mean to sound disloyal toward them. I just need to know what happened and who died. It is so hard to hear but not really know," she said.

"Shall I sit up for a while with you until you feel better?" Isaac asked.

"Oh...no...I'll be all right. I want to think about this. I will go to bed and probably will sleep after a while," Samantha said.

"Maybe you need Catherine to sit with you. Can I tell her to come and try to help you feel better? She would, you know," Isaac said.

"I know she would, but I would feel guilty to keep her up since she has to wake in the early morning to nurse baby Henry. I am going to bed and so should you," Samantha said.

She really didn't want Catherine to lose her sleep and besides she could think about each member of her family until she fell asleep. "Thanks for letting me know, Isaac."

Samantha was upset but with only the last name, it could be any one of the eight members of her family. She thought of each one of them with love as she let go and went on to visualize the next one. It couldn't be either of her parents. They were both necessary to take care of the rest of the family. It could not be Jonathan. It could not be allowed, not possibly. They had become quite happy with each other as siblings and they would soon pick right back up with more love than ever. Matthew had become so helpful to Father and he was needed, too. Her three little sisters were sweet and loving. They each needed a chance to grow up and find happiness. She could still find happiness herself and be there to help them along. They would need someone to understand them in a particular way like Gram had understood her.

She didn't have one she was willing to lose. She longed to get to Ohio Country. She curled into a ball to think of her grandmother, Priscilla Crow. She could almost smell the rose and thyme sachets Gram made. Gram is not ancient, maybe in her mid-sixties, but it is the most logical that it may be her. She didn't want it to be anyone. She wondered if it would be easier or harder to know which one it was? She fell asleep with her foreboding thoughts, which would be present again as soon as her eyes opened.

Samantha wrote another line in her journal when the house began to stir with people. She had saved newspaper accounts of Dr. Goodson's death and the trial of Cretia. Her journal contained a personal parallel account of it, also, and now it would include her lament and love for each member of her family. The journal had no answers, just the recording of her anguish about who had died and how foreboding and unthinkable it was to try to believe it from a distance.

She smelled coffee and was thankful for her family right here. Auntie Geneva loved her and quite possibly Uncle Percy did, too. It would help to feel Auntie's arms around her. She went to the kitchen and Auntie already knew her mind. Samantha hugged Auntie and felt grateful to have her caring arms. She saw the dishes in the dishpan already used by Uncle Percy and Isaac. Isaac had informed Auntie about Samantha's bad news when he ate breakfast. He knew how important Auntie was to her.

"Auntie, it's so hard to lose people you care about, first Cretia, now Gram, or probably Gram, but I can't be sure," Samantha said.

"Just being alive and human brings pain to our door and not one of us wants to lose someone we love. You know I lost my brother, Gowdy Lee. I don't forget, but I don't speak about it because it is so hurtful just like Cretia's death. It stays inside my heart like it does with yours. It's the only thing we have left to do. We honor them by remembering them with love," Auntie said.

"I won't forget how I loved Cretia and Gram," Samantha said.

Catherine and two-year-old Margaret came into the kitchen for breakfast. Little Margaret was happy to climb up on Samantha to sit as long as her father was not available. Samantha kissed her cheek as she held her. Margaret liked Samantha's long hair and pulled it around her own face. "She is always doing something to fidget," Catherine said and laughed. "I really need a bassinet handy to lay the baby in so I can help cook."

"I have it covered, Miss Catherine. No need to worry about putting that sweet child down," Auntie said. She cheerfully put food in front of Samantha, Catherine, and Margaret. Auntie Geneva's own food was last. Samantha finished eating and was washing the dishes. Catherine wanted to help, too, but couldn't without provision for her baby, other than her arms. She stood and used one hand to rinse and drain dishes.

When Auntie was through eating, she was prepared to take over the dishes but Samantha continued. Catherine handed her baby to Auntie Geneva and said, "Rest your feet," and Auntie did. She could not help rocking the baby and a slow humming could not be helped either. Baby boy Hogan went to sleep under the comforting care of Auntie for the first time, but not to be the last. When he was soundly asleep, Auntie Geneva asked, "What do you call this child, Miss Catherine?"

"We have waited to name him but we are trying to decide what it will be. He will soon be quite old enough to have an identity since he will be one-month-old," Catherine said.

"We remember how long ago he was born, right Auntie?" Samantha said, smiling.

"I believe we were both there and have good memories," Auntie said. The three laughed, recounting the birth when all three were present.

Samantha went to inventory more of the house contents to single out what would be sold. "Auntie Geneva, the kitchen stuff will be last and only with your help so I am sure of what we have to take with us. I couldn't do this room without you," she said.

"It can wait until the very last, Miss S'manthy," Auntie Geneva said. "Some pots cannot be packed until after canning, anyway."

Catherine laughed. "We can't forgo canning," she said.

"Forget? I am very much in favor of it, forgetting that is," Samantha said as she joined Catherine's happy mood.

Samantha's problem about one room, which she could not bring herself to go into alone, kept her from opening that door. It was the door which had held a monster behind it until he died. Dr. Goodson was gone, but her dread returned when she wanted to go in there to list items. She planned, at a later time, to ask someone to go through that door with her.

She avoided the closed room at the end of the hall. There were many other rooms in which to do inventory and add the contents to her list. She could work in the room that the very ill Eunice Goodson had occupied until her death. Methodical work would get it done. It was no small job, proven when she opened one large closet with gowns and each of them had matching shoes. They would auction off easier than furniture she believed. It crossed her mind that Auntie Geneva and Catherine could wear them, but it was not likely they would want to. That could be done only with the newest ones. They had come from off the ship at dock by the Potomac River near Mt. Vernon, as brand-new and had never been worn by anyone.

Samantha tried to determine which ones they were. It was the easiest job she had as it turned out. They were still wrapped in paper and hung in the middle of the second closet.

Eunice had been too ill on return home from Mt. Vernon's social season, to consider fashions that had been ordered when she was completely well. Samantha laid six paper wrapped dresses on the bed and wrote simple descriptions of all the others in the closets. The room was an afternoon of work and she was happy to have it accomplished. She would show Catherine and Auntie Geneva another day, to admire the gowns, but she was too tired now.

She needed a rest and went into her own room and lay down to study from the medical book she hadn't opened yet. There were pages on apothecary, medicinal concoctions, and home remedies. She read slowly and doubled back over almost every page so she could try to learn it well. It was slow, but methodical learning, which she was determined to master. Samantha was forced to consult the index, and often a dictionary for explanations of medical terms for which she had no idea of their meanings.

Determination would be hers day after day as she made progress. Often, a thick volume was draped across her for a late afternoon nap and she was glad that falling asleep happened in the afternoon rather than at night by oil lamp. Falling asleep with an oil lamp or candle burning would not do. She was reminded of hearing it said many times by her mother that it would not be a grown-up action. The afternoon nap always gave her a second wind and made it safer when she went back to reading each night.

Black streaks were present on the glass globe each morning as the smoke left its mark when she blew it out at night. She polished globes after breakfast each day from her night lamp and from each one used by the household the evening before. Auntie Geneva had given up saying she would do it. Samantha and Catherine were not putting all of the work on her and Auntie was starting to like the idea.

Samantha had read and studied nearly a quarter of the heavy medical volume until the afternoon when papers and envelopes fell to the floor. They dropped from somewhere in the thick book, which had swallowed them months before and held them fast, unnoticed. The volume lay there on the rug as she bent to pick up the paper she could not pull her eyes from. She knew it was the stolen note lost months ago when the apron pocket ripped.

Her hands shook as she read the familiar words of Corporal Daniel Sutter. Tears welled up as she finished reading the words, which still warmed her cheeks and made her heart beat with pleasure. Her affection for him was no less than it was when she first met him at Yorktown battle camp. Her fond feelings for him had heightened when the corporal gave the message meant for her, to her brother, Jonathan, to hold until her return from Mt. Vernon. She placed it in her pocket and bent to pick up her brother's hand-drawn map along with three envelopes, each one addressed to Miss Samantha Crow. Her unashamed tears competed with sobs when she examined each return address.

Auntie Geneva had been attracted to her door at the sound of sobbing. She stepped in and asked, "Miss S'manthy, what troubles you so, dear girl?" She saw the envelopes but had no comprehension of their worth since she could not read.

Catherine stepped in. "Where are these from, Samantha?"

The sobs stopped and turned to anger, which threatened to choke Samantha. "Dr. Goodson stole my mail and hid it without ever telling me I had letters from home and from Martha Washington," she said. Her fists were tight balls of white knuckles with her arms stiff at her sides.

"Miss S'manthy, you have to lie down. You've made yourself sick, child," Auntie said.

Samantha slumped against Auntie and Catherine as they guided her to lie back on the cushions. She let go of her grasp on the envelopes and Catherine laid them beside her.

Auntie brought a sip of water for Samantha with a wet cloth for her hot cheeks and forehead. She understood emotions perfectly and both women were concerned for Samantha.

"I'm all right now," Samantha said. "I have not often been so angered, but I should have been past it since Dr. Goodson is dead and gone. It seemed like he was right here with his hate and laughing at me with his control,"

"You can't let the devil doctor overtake you again, Miss S'manthy," Auntie Geneva said.

"I won't let him affect me so badly again, Auntie," Samantha promised.

"Forget all about Dr. Goodson and be glad for settlement of the estate soon, so you can leave this place, which reminds you of him. You'll probably be quite happy when you read your letters," Catherine said.

Samantha sat up. She must read them and treasure them. "I need to enjoy reading them right now," she said.

Auntie and Catherine walked to the door. "We hope they are letters full of good sentiments and be sure to let us know if you need us, please," Catherine said.

Chapter 5

The Letters
Found in June 1783

Samantha sat down to read the letters and noticed that each envelope was without its wax seal and the flaps were loose. Dr. Goodson had read every one of them. She refused to be angered again and reminded herself that he could not hurt her from the grave. He had no more control over her, not even to make her fly into a rage. She mentally turned her back on his past insults.

Martha Washington's letter was first as Samantha remembered that Martha had promised to write if she was able to send information of importance on the whereabouts of Corporal Daniel Sutter. She thought it curious and then worrisome that according to the date on the top of the letter, it had been written so long ago and was dated five months before. So it was written five months after she and Martha last spoke. Samantha dwelled on it.

It isn't Martha's fault that the letters were stolen and missing another five months. What will all of the wasted time mean for information about Corporal Sutter? Why must I think of trouble even before I read it? She opened it and began.

~~*~~

February 1, 1783

My Dear Friend, Samantha,

Five months have passed since we last embraced as friends on your departure from Mt. Vernon. I did not forget that I promised to write you with information if General Washington had been able to locate your Corporal Daniel Sutter.

Corporal Sutter is stationed in New York State with General Washington where they wait with only the remnant of 2,500 men of the Continental Army. The wait, which I believe I mentioned to you in person, is for The Treaty of Paris to be signed in France under the efforts of Ben Franklin and others. It is expected within this year or first half of next year. It will formalize the victory won at Yorktown. Then every country involved will be willing to sell, or trade, or barter their already claimed land west of the Mississippi River. It insures that colonies will not be limited to settlement only east of the Mississippi River. Many more settlers will feel confident to move west as well as north to settle when peace is an absolute, signed on paper.

The final signature on the treaty will signal the British presence to sail out of NYC harbor with many of the traitor Loyalists and their families on board. That is when General Washington can retire from the great theater of action and return to his beloved Mt. Vernon. That date is eagerly awaited for word to arrive from across the vast waters and it seems at a snail's pace for those of us who wait for our soldiers.

Corporal Sutter has been among the last faithful enlisted men standing by General Washington within his remnant army and will retire with a five-year pension at full pay to start his civilian life. Congress had passed a bill to make it half pay for life, but it was commuted to the five years for all enlisted men. Plans have changed before but tentatively the army will plan on going home or making a home when the Peace Treaty is final. Can you imagine my happiness here at Mt. Vernon when that happens?

George spoke with Corporal Sutter who said he had written to you on January 1, 1783, about the possibility of coming to get you. That letter came back with a red message across the front saying: Address of No Such Person: Miss Samantha Crow *Your name was scribbled on the line.*

So, now I write with great hope that you receive this and to tell you that Corporal Sutter will muster out in the vague time frame as mentioned all ready. I have let George know that your family was to move to Licking Springs in Ohio Country this year and that you could be there now. I know what your heart was, but even these things can change.

I will arrive back at Mt. Vernon on May 15 as I always do, to start the summer there with Nellie and my grandchildren.

Please advise me of what I may tell George on behalf of Corporal Sutter that he may have your desire known.

I pray that you make haste in writing.

*With Great Fondness and Friendship,
Martha Washington*

~~*~~

Samantha was stunned at the news of Martha's letter and dismayed, wondering why Daniel's letter had been refused and returned to him? She had been right here all along. Did Dr. Goodson have the new blacksmith turn the letter away or did the smithy just have no idea that her name was Samantha Crow? He could have asked anyone in town so that couldn't be the reason. She must write something to Martha right away at Mt. Vernon since her dear friend would remain there now.

Father's letter was opened second. Her heart was wide open to love and the gratitude of having the writing of her father in front of her. It was dated a month after Eunice Goodson had died and acknowledged that Dr. Goodson had written that it was an inconvenient time to be able to plan a trip north to Ohio Country.

December 10, 1782
Dear Daughter, Samantha,

We were pleased to receive your letter along with that of Edgar Goodson's, which informed us of the unfortunate death of his wife, Eunice, in November. We are proud to know that you were of help to take such delicate care of her. We do understand that Dr. Goodson's grief would delay a move to Ohio Country. We await your spring arrival.

All in this family are well at present, including Grandmother Crow, who helps within this family with all of her gentle love and care for the younger children.

Our plan for staking a claim at Licking Springs was delayed when we arrived at the southern bank of the Ohio River where the Scioto River intersects it. Surprisingly, the land grants are not ready to be claimed yet until after the Treaty of Paris is signed. Many settlers have gone ahead north anyway into Ohio Country and some have lost their lives to the Shawnee tribe.

We were quick to repair an unoccupied cabin of four rooms to contain this large family for the winter and will be safer here at the river intersection while we wait for progress and a more reliable time. I expect to be overwhelmed with work in the spring when we continue into Ohio Country. I will clear land when we finally make a claim. It will insure that the sun can get through to a garden your mother has planned. She counts on your help when you arrive in the spring, a few short months.

No one has the same information about the number of acres that a militiaman or former enlisted man can claim in the Virginia Military District to be set aside. Rumors are so different that none is believed reliable.

Hunting is bountiful with lots of fresh game to be found. Between Jonathan and me bringing down big game, we eat plenty of meat. Matthew has made us proud with added small game by his accurate shooting.

We all wish you a Merry Christmas.

With Love from Family,
Your Father, William Crow

~~*~~

December 10, 1782
My Dear Sister, Samantha,

I am sorry that your arrival here to join the family has been put off for next spring. Since we can't have you for our Christmas present, I wish you a Merry Christmas. I will have to hold onto a gift I made for you as it is yours the first chance that I see you.

68

I let Father explain where and why we are at the Ohio and Scioto River intersection, southern side of the Ohio River. I was already working and waiting here where all settlers would stay to wait for the signed treaty and the military tracts to be surveyed. I am sorry some went into Ohio Country and lost their scalps and their lives to the Shawnee. We won't be foolish and will wait here at the intersect point.

You will need a coat in Ohio Country for winter and I tell you the snow is beautiful but cold. It is a help in tracking deer and other plentiful animals. My time is spent hunting or working for the freight rail line. By day, I unload salt from railroad cars and by night I play night watchman over the same cars. It is a short rail line of a few miles to move salt in bulk down to the place where it will be packed and distributed. The newly invented steam engine pulls it and I can see where the future could hold plans for longer sections of track, maybe from state to state to carry passengers. It could put horse pulled coaches out of business. Father says I dream big but may have something there.

Of course, I wonder and hope your corporal comes for you in the scheme of his plans for married life. I hold no doubt that none other took his eye or his heart from you.

You Remain in my Highest Esteem.

Love, Your Brother,
Jonathan Crow

~~*~~

Samantha held the correspondence notes close to her heart as she sank back into her soft cushions. Happiness was tempered by worry because of the amount of time gone by. The first letter she must write would be to Martha at Mt. Vernon. She would explain what seemed prudent, but most of all Martha could get the word to General Washington and Corporal Sutter of her whereabouts and her pleasure in knowing that Corporal Daniel Sutter would still be hers. Samantha went to the library desk to compose letters. She wasted no time in writing, as it was her urgent task. She wrote with a thankful heart and mind.

~~*~~

June 30, 1783

My Dear Friend, Martha,

I am grateful for your letter dated February 1, 1783. I received it only now on the date above and you must guess at how upsetting this is to me. I am writing without delay, at my first possible moment to let you know that I have never lost heart for thought of Corporal Daniel Sutter. I am very proud of his faithful conduct in the service of General Washington's Continentals.

I must tell you that my family is settled in the south of Ohio Country in the interim, temporarily until the Treaty of Paris is signed and the Virginia Military Tracts become designated in Ohio Country. They have been waiting since last fall of 1782 at the Ohio and Scioto River intersection. I have recently heard a reliable rumor that a person with the last name of Crow died there, but I do not know which one. You can imagine my distress.

I stayed behind in Virginia to become a nurse for Mrs. Eunice Goodson, who never got well and she died last November. There is too much to relate about all that has happened, but to summarize, Dr. Edgar Goodson died March 11, 1783, and his slave, Cretia, was tried and hanged for his murder. I will leave other details to be told in person or not at all.

I trust you are enjoying Nellie and the children. Please convey my best to Nellie.

I will leave Virginia at the end of August in good company of friends and expect to be in my family's presence by the Ohio River in the middle of September.

Thank you for helping make the connection with Corporal Sutter as it means everything to me.

I hold you in my highest esteem.

In Fond Remembrance of Friendship,
Miss Samantha Crow

~~*~~

June 30, 1783

Dear Father and Mother,

I have just this day received your letter dated December 10, 1782, sending me pleasant Christmas wishes.

I heard a rumor that there was a death in the Crow family but remain unaware who it is. It is with dread that I tell you how sorry I am to hear of it. I am anguished at losing even one of our family members.

I have many things to tell you, but some of it can wait until I arrive at the Ohio and Scioto River connection in the middle of September. Then I will share newspaper accounts and my daily journal of all that has happened.

You knew Eunice Goodson was deceased but add now that Dr. Goodson is also deceased. Information about that is too much to explain in a letter.

I will be traveling north with friends, in safe company and you do not need to worry about my safety.

I will wait for Corporal Sutter at the Ohio River intersection where you are located if he has not come to Virginia first. Martha Washington was helpful in getting General Washington to locate Corporal Sutter and in conveying our same intentions to each other. I trust that he and I will be together late this year or within half of the next.

I will keep all of you in my heart and in my prayers. I love you all.

Your Daughter,
Samantha Crow

~~*~~

June 10, 1783

Dear Brother, Jonathan,

I have only now received your December letter on the date above, I am sorry to say. I am glad to have Father's and Martha Washington's letters as well, but there was also a long lapse from when all of the letters were here without my knowledge. I will explain why when I see you.

The letter I wrote Father says the same about my planned travel with friends and our expected arrival at the Ohio Scioto intersection by the middle of September.

Martha Washington let me know that Corporal Sutter had a letter returned to him, which he sent to me. I have hastily written her to get the word to Daniel that I will leave here by the first of September. He will be able to locate me with my family there if not before I leave lower Virginia. I appreciate your hopeful words on my plans with him as my mind is set the same as his.

You are indeed working hard and to your credit. I am proud of you. The steam engine train surely is a new-fangled marvel and you need to be careful working around it. I am sure I read your thoughts on that remark that it was a feminine thought to be worrying.

Please know that I say it because I miss you and of course our family very much.

I will keep in mind that you have a gift for me and will be more than happy to receive it. I hold you in my highest esteem.

With Love, Your Sister,
Samantha Crow

~~*~~

Samantha leaned back from her concentration of letter writing to sigh with relief for the finish. She hadn't been able to bring herself to sign her name as Widow Goodson or even Samantha Goodson. She planned to explain later after traveling north. Samantha had not once looked away from her urgent mission of writing the letters. When Catherine looked in the library door to tell her that supper was ready, it was a surprise for Samantha to learn that the afternoon was gone.

"Thank you, Catherine. I lost track of time with the necessary task of writing three letters that will have to be sent right away."

"I believe Auntie and I know who they are for but Isaac has not been here to know that you found letters, which prompted your flurry of writing in answer. He has news, too, and wants to gather all of us together right after supper if we will all make time," Catherine said.

Samantha smiled. "Of course, we will make time."

Chapter 6

Progress Made
End of June 1783

Supper was finished and all food and dishes put away. Isaac stood while he waited, anxious to begin. He wasted no time in saying, "Catherine has something to report before I get into the reason for this meeting."

Catherine stood. "I am happy to announce the name we have chosen for baby boy Hogan. We will enter his name into the family page in the front of our bible, which shall be Henry Otis Mosher Hogan. He is named after both of our fathers,"

Little Margaret clapped her hands and they were all delighted to see Samantha join her. Catherine and Isaac were pleased as Percy and Geneva added their clapping approval.

"Before we get to your business, Isaac, can we tell you of the happening here this afternoon in your absence?" Catherine said.

"I yield the floor," Isaac said.

"Samantha made a discovery in the pages of the medical book she has been studying. She can relate what happened next," Catherine said.

"Three letters fell out of the thick book and I have also written three letters in answer, which must be sent at once," Samantha said.

"The letters must be to you since you are answering them, but from whom?" Isaac asked.

"They are from Mrs. Washington and my father and brother," Samantha said. "I believe I can sum the letters up to let you know what they are all about without taking too long." She had everyone's complete attention. When she had finished they all congratulated her on the good news of hearing from family.

"We are all the benefactors of the letters being found because the Ohio Country destination is important to each one of us here. You must be glad for the critical word about your corporal, too, Samantha," Isaac said with his broad smile. His happy look must have been a signal for Little Margaret to clap and everyone's mood made them willing to clap their hands again with her.

"Good news for Samantha makes us all happy and gives us reason to cheer," Isaac said. Little Margaret was not ready to stop the applause and they all enjoyed her exuberance.

"Percy, I believe you have information that requires our input," Isaac said.

"Yes, Sir, I do," Percy said. He turned to Samantha. "I found a big wagon today at a low price if you want to consider it, Miss S'manthy. It is a lower price because it needs a new tongue made to pull it, which I can make better than the one that broke. Leroy can help me deliver a new limb to that farm and repair it there so we can hook mules up to it and bring it back here," he said.

"I think we'll take it on your word, Uncle Percy, and thank you for finding it," Samantha said. Little Margaret clapped as if she knew it would be well received, and it was. They all clapped with her.

"The clapping is over now, Margaret," Isaac said as he held onto her little hands.

"One point, Samantha, the date on your father's and brother's letters, what were they?" Isaac said.

"They were December, last year. I failed to mention their Christmas wish written to me or you would have known," Samantha said.

"It was too early then since hearing of those two deaths, which happened this year and has no relationship to your father's letter saying that your grandmother was well. She was fine then, sorry I mentioned it, Samantha. I don't mean to upset you," Isaac said.

"We all need to be able to speak freely and keep every one of us informed if only to clarify," Samantha said, "So I'm not upset."

"I have exact information about the auction date we could choose according to when the auctioneer will be able to work in this area. He gave two dates to choose from, August 15 and August 28. We need to pick one immediately to schedule selling the contents of your house. I suggest we choose August 28 since we still have your legal matters in the process and the end not quite in sight. There is another reason we can't leave sooner. A trailblazer, Grant Macon, is only available at the end of August," Isaac added.

"I agree with the 28th of August if Auntie Geneva and Uncle Percy think we can do it by then," Samantha said. "There are the gardens to consider."

"We both agree," Uncle Percy said. "We are all better off having a date and working toward something particular," he said with a broad smile. Auntie Geneva couldn't help wearing the same smile and Little Margaret could not help seeing that it was a reason to clap.

"This child has a contagious happiness about her," Auntie Geneva said, but adult clapping did not resume.

"Isaac, did I hear you right? You only mentioned selling the contents of the house, but I must sell the house, too," Samantha said.

"We will auction the house if we have to, but I'm talking with a possible buyer now, a doctor who may move here and be able to buy it. I have to make an appointment with you now to allow him to inspect and consider it. The ideal setup for a doctor's exam room is ready to use, so he knows he would have immediate use. He needs to determine if it will be workable for two families since he has a new wife. His parents will come, too, and help buy it if he reports that it is suitable," Isaac said.

"When do they want to see it, Isaac?" Samantha asked.

"If Dr. Manville can look at it tomorrow, he can head on back to notify his wife and parents of his findings. If not tomorrow, then he will not be back for two weeks. I took the liberty of telling him that the ladies of this house keep it in excellent shape and that I would let him know tomorrow morning if he can inspect it for his consideration," Isaac said.

"Oh, dear. We should clean all the drapes and remove the rugs to beat them. They are overdue, Miss S'manthy," Auntie Geneva said.

"No, oh no, nothing so energetic is required and it seems appropriate to show it to him. When he looks and if he accepts it to make an offer, it still does not need to be done," Isaac said.

"He is right, Auntie. Don't think up more work if we do not need to do it," Catherine said. Samantha nodded in definite agreement.

"What time do you want to allow for his appraisal., Samantha?" Isaac asked.

"I believe tomorrow at 11:00 a.m. would let us do quite enough to feel confident of a dust free parlor. But, Isaac, to allow this timing for his visit, I will need your help tonight to open the room formerly occupied by Dr. Goodson. I find it impossible to go in there alone," Samantha said.

"Of course, I will and then we can decide if we are ready for a possible buyer. Can everyone wait a bit while we check the room?" Isaac asked.

"We will wait," Uncle Percy said.

Isaac transferred his sleeping little girl into Auntie's arms and he started toward the room with a lamp in his hand. Samantha followed down the hallway behind him. Isaac opened the door and stepped inside ahead of Samantha. He set the lamp down on a bureau at the side of the room. "Well, what do you see? What can I help you with in here?" he said.

"I want to open drawers and chests and everything in here to see what we find. Maybe there will be something important and maybe not," Samantha said. "But I need to do it."

"You are right," Isaac said. He opened each drawer of the chest of drawers and it was predictable, containing personal clothing items for summer and the bottom drawers for winter wear. There were a dozen pair of socks at least and a few long night shirts. Isaac ran his hands under the contents of each drawer, but they contained only clothes.

"I believe these garments will be given away. I think if we leave the door open now, maybe Auntie and Catherine can come inside with me in daylight hours to clear the room out when we are ready," Samantha said. "And we will need to place a quilt over the ticking."

"I agree but let me check on something I wonder about," Isaac said. He stepped over to the mattress and pulled the ticking away from the headboard. "This catches my eye with unusually broad framing to hold a wider board near the headboard. It is different on this end of the bed...curious." He pushed on the end of the board where the mattress had previously rested. It did not move. "Hmm, I thought it would flip up," he said. He tapped along the length of it. "It sounds empty." He pushed on it every few inches. "Sometimes these are made hollow to use as a hiding place, you know," Isaac said.

"No...I did not know. I never heard of such a thing," Samantha said.

"Hold on...we have movement here," Isaac said. He pushed down a foot from the outside edge and the board flipped up. He picked it out of its place, covering a trough, and laid it on the mattress. Samantha watched as he pulled a long musket out. "Nothing very surprising here," Isaac said. He reached in again to pull a bag of black gun powder out. "Now let me show you another place I suspect of having a surprising niche near the side. If I'm right, there must be some way to get in there. Can you bring the light closer?" Isaac asked.

Samantha brought the lamp and he tapped along the end until it swung out. He reached inside to pull out a box, which had fit perfectly inside.

"What do we have here?" Isaac said. He folded the lid back to lie open flat. His low whistle announced his approval of a small gun nestled in a velvet form. "This is a ladies' gun. Any lady would feel safe holding this security in her pocket."

"I have never seen anything like it," Samantha said.

"People with means have them and you will soon be a woman of means when I get finances in order for you," he said. He picked it up and checked it for load. "It is loaded with black powder...should be safe to handle if you are careful and want to try it in your hand.."

Samantha picked it up from the velvet lined box where he had replaced it. "I like the small size of it," she said.

"It's an English Flintlock Pocket Pistol," Isaac said. He laughed when she slipped it in her pocket underneath the plume of her navy and gold dress.

She smiled. "I am now a lady."

Isaac's head went back in a hearty laugh.

"Catherine and Geneva can help in here tomorrow morning, but I'm not convinced there is anything needed," Isaac said. He slipped the musket back inside the long slot along with a bag of gunpowder. The board was pushed back into place and Isaac shoved the mattress back where it had been. "It's out of sight for tomorrow," Isaac said.

"I'm going out the door first," Samantha said as she picked up the lamp to go.

Uncle Percy was sitting there watching Geneva hum a spiritual to a sleeping child and Catherine was as sleepy as baby Henry in her arms. Isaac reached for Little Margaret and Auntie Geneva stood up to make the transfer into Isaac's arms. "Thank you, Auntie Geneva," he said. "I know you folks want to get some rest and we'll see you in the morning but for tonight progress has been made."

"We will get an early start," Auntie Geneva said. "We all want to make sure we haven't overlooked anything before Dr. Manville comes by here."

"Goodnight Auntie," Samantha said with a hug.

~~*~~

Breakfast was always a good start and as they finished, Isaac stood up. "I don't believe any of you are aware that a house sells best if it is empty of people when a prospective buyer looks it over. You can bring the children to the office to wait, Catherine."

"I will come with her to help with the little ones," Auntie said.

"Auntie, if you want time to go to your cabin, I can help Catherine," Samantha said.

"Miss S'manthy, beg your pardon, but Miss Catherine will be safer with me, but you should come, too, "Auntie said.

Samantha wrinkled her nose and shook her head. "It's not fair for people to be quite so unreasonable. I was always safe around here before. The town's people seem to have forgotten that General George Washington gave me a horse and he considers me a patriot, since I helped at the battle of Yorktown. I may take a ride on my horse, Auntie, but I can decide when we leave the house later," Samantha said.

Isaac had to weigh in with his concern. "You need to stay within your fenced pasture acres to ride. It's not safe for you to be out alone on the road, Samantha. I'll return at 11:00 a.m. with our buyer. One last thing; I did write a formal letter to request your knife return from the sheriff's office and will let you know when I have a reply."

"Thank you," Samantha said.

Isaac went out the door and his steps grew quieter as he walked further away down the boardwalk.

"Catherine, will you help me make a wax seal on these three envelopes, please? I have never done it and I need to get it right and send them on their way. They can be sent when we leave the house," Samantha said.

"Miss S'manthy, the letters should be taken to Mr. Isaac to send from his office so you can avoid this unfriendly town. You need to be careful of troublemakers," Uncle Percy said.

"I will take your wise advice, Uncle Percy," Samantha said. She felt of the flintlock pistol through the cloth of her dress. She wondered why it made her feel safer when she didn't know much about shooting it? She thought of what Isaac told her that it had black powder loaded and if it becomes cocked and the trigger pulled, it will propel a small lead ball forward at something or somebody. It was not all that different than when she shot her brother, Jonathan's, Brown Bess Musket.

Chapter 7

Unending Work
July and August 1783

July had gone fast with continuous work. It left no time for leisurely pleasures for anyone in the household. Riding, knitting, and reading was left aside. All things were being made ready for the new owners to move into Goodson House. Not one of them felt sad to think of leaving, and Samantha was happy with anticipation. It had been easy to sign papers to sell Goodson House to Dr. Manville who would take it over on the morning of September first. She had money from a bank account in her name and could buy anything she wanted. What she wanted was Corporal Daniel Sutter and to reach Ohio Country and the arms of her family. They had no idea what Samantha had endured.

It would not be possible to start the journey north until after the hardest month of all, August, which stretched in front of them. Food had to be canned, dried, pickled, salted, and smoked. All preservation methods were necessary so they would have ample food for the winter when they reached Ohio Country.

The scheduled sale of household contents would be last, but there was also constant work every day to get ready for auction on August 28th.

Samantha longed to ride her horse, to read more in the medical volumes, and to daydream of idle reverie and hopes for the future if she pleased. "Auntie Geneva, there is so much unending work to accomplish. Will we ever be finished?" she asked in her weariness of what she regarded as duty, duty, duty.

"Miss S'manthy, we will get it all done and if we were not going anywhere, the work would be the same in order to put food by for the winter. We have to eat in Virginia the same as we do in Ohio Country. Makes no difference where we are as far as having to eat," Auntie said.

Catherine laughed. "That simplifies it, Auntie. We just get it done all the while we are helping each other in pleasant company."

Samantha had to laugh, too. She was guilty of wishing all the work was over, but

Auntie had a way of putting it in simple terms. "It makes it easier to do when you put it like that, Auntie, and Catherine is right about doing it together," she said.

"At least we don't have to remove heavy drapes or floor coverings or anything in the exam room. It was good that you could sell all of those items with the house to the new owner," Catherine said to Samantha.

"Yes, you are right. We have to look at the work we have saved, since we pulled off a smart sale," Samantha said. "Another thing we can do is to use the waiting room to store items in, those which we are taking with us, but don't have to use now. They will be out of our way and will also be next to the side door to be loaded on wagons when it is time."

"I have reconsidered and think some of the kettles can be stored in there, Miss S'manthy. But you and I need to decide on what goes and what sells at auction from the kitchen," Auntie Geneva said.

"I have clothes that I can't wear in this heat and I could pack them," Catherine said.

"The smartest way to put items in the room would be to stack each family's belongings in their own section. That way when a wagon is pulled into the alley for loading, we don't have to sort the room for what belongs in each family's wagon," Catherine said.

"That is a perfect way to do it. We do not own much, Miss S'manthy, so I think pots and pans can go in our wagon to save room for your things in your wagon," Auntie Geneva said.

"We will all have the bottoms of our wagons packed with preserved or canned food, like my parents did, and then the bed frame and mattress over the top of that. If we pack the Hogan wagon first, then mine, we will see if the pots and pans need to go in yours, Auntie," Samantha said.

"We are all agreed then on tight packing to make the most of space," Catherine said. "We will inform the men of our discussion before we have another meeting so they can add ideas if they can come up with something more."

"They cannot come up with better ideas than we do," Catherine said, "just added ideas." All three of them laughed together.

"I'm reminded of something," Samantha said. "I want both of you to come and look at some brand-new dresses, which belonged to Mrs. Goodson. They came off the ship from England. When she arrived home, she was quite ill and they were hung in the closet and forgotten." They were all happy for a lighter note and a break from work in the kitchen with a hot brick oven. Canning was hot work and they were quite ready to take a short rest.

The elegant frocks were laid out on the bed still in the tissue-paper wrappers. "If we are careful, we can remove the paper so it will be replaced when we decide what to do with these. It is my idea that we may each be able to have two new dresses to take to Ohio Country with us," Samantha said. "We may want to wrap them back for protection."

Catherine laughed. "You are so generous, Samantha, but you can keep all of them, of course."

"I can't use that many gowns and besides it would be lovely for each of us to have them," Samantha said. Carefully, they peeled paper off to each side. "Let's peel open the other three so we know what each one looks like," Samantha said. When she opened the next one, she knew she wanted that one for herself, a beautiful baby blue velvet plumed skirt over white satin with white lace trim. "Oh...this one is claimed," Samantha said. "Now you each pick one."

"You can pick first, Auntie Geneva," Catherine said. They turned toward her when no reply came.

Auntie had tears streaming down her face. "You can't mean it, Miss S'manthy. I never had a dress like that. Where would I wear it?"

Catherine and Samantha put their arms around her. "Why Auntie Geneva, you will wear it wherever you like in Ohio Country or anywhere you care to go, free to do as you wish," Samantha said.

Catherine added, "I think you will get used to wearing beautiful clothes, Auntie, so pick one." They waited and Auntie could not reach for a dress. She could not decide.

Samantha asked, "Do you like this yellow and brown combo or maybe the rose and gray? I would rather you pick your own instead of my choice for you," she said.

"I can see that the yellow with brown looks attractive next to your sweet face, Auntie," Catherine said. She picked it up and pressed it against Geneva. "Look in the mirror, Auntie."

Auntie turned and her wide eyes looked like she would never believe it was hers. "It's a bit too big," she said.

Samantha and Catherine laughed. "You can take a nip and tuck for yourself now instead of for a mistress," Samantha said. "You are a great seamstress, Auntie. And now I will be selfish and pick another one." She reached for a bone color satin with white velvet cascading gathers on the back and sides of the skirt. "I love this one, too," Samantha said. She had a particular idea for the use of the dress. "Catherine, pick one."

Catherine picked up a purple velvet and floated dream-like toward the mirror. Samantha and Auntie clapped for her dramatics. "It is the perfect choice for you," Samantha said.

The cries of baby Henry broke the spell of high-fashion decisions. "I must go but, Auntie, please pick another one and I will be delighted with the last one left," Catherine said as she left the room. Auntie chose the gray with pink. It left the green velvet over mauve satin for Catherine.

"I will not wear these here so I may as well put them in the waiting room with the medical books and black bag of tools," Samantha said. "I must pick two of the used dresses to take to Mother. They may as well be new since they have no signs of wear."

Auntie spoke up. "The dresses were for perfect appearance with no work ever done by Eunice. They could not show wear and tear."

It was only meant for truth as usual from Auntie, no meanness intended. "I could not possibly wear them here either," Auntie Geneva said. "I will start my new life in Ohio Country wearing them. Thank you, Miss S'manthy." They carried dresses into the waiting room for later. Catherine's gowns were also taken to storage. Samantha gathered two more from the closet and placed them in her designated corner of the waiting room.

Samantha did not say it, but she believed there would be no use to take a garment for Gram as she believed Grandmother was no more.

Auntie Geneva and Samantha started one more canner full of mixed vegetables, which would be perfect added to a pot of chicken and dumplings for one-pot meals. It had to come to a boil and be timed, which could be done while they cleaned up the kitchen. Samantha was exhausted and thought about earlier days when she had helped Mother and Gram. Now she knew they were easier in comparison and longed for a more carefree time again, or was she imagining it had been easier now that she missed them? She didn't know, but she was sure of being tired.

They were glad that supper was the lightest meal of the day and not a lot to fuss over. Buttermilk biscuits and cider were prepared. The few leftover chicken pieces from midday dinner would be finished off by the men. Catherine came in with her wide-awake children. Margaret was happy to have attention from Auntie and Samantha, but only because her father was not yet present.

The long days of drying and canning food were spent in harmony between the three women as they felt pride in the progress they made in putting up food for the winter. They talked again about how they would have it loaded in the three wagon bottoms and the wooden bed frames placed just above it with a mattress for nighttime stops. Percy, Leroy, and Isaac had measured the three beds to be taken and agreed on the plan. They had also brought the small bed from the farm for baby Henry to lie in. It made Catherine's days easier.

Busy days left Samantha with only the evenings to read and study. She allowed herself only one hour to enjoy it because she was too tired to trust herself longer for fear she would fall asleep with a lighted lamp and cause a fire.

It was interesting to read about snake bite and how to treat it. She went over it again since it was a practical knowledge to have. Use of a knife for the procedure reminded her that she needed the medium size knife back for her set and she would ask Isaac if the sheriff had replied yet.

Samantha knew she would not be done with the books for a long time after she reached Ohio Country and then they would serve for reference. She continued to cherish her letters, her brother's hand-drawn map, and Daniel Sutter's love note the last thing before she fell asleep each night.

It was the middle of August when Isaac summoned Samantha to the parlor for a private consultation in midday. "Why just me?" she asked after they went into the sitting room.

"I have news for you alone and you can decide if any of it can be shared," Isaac said. "Let me advise you as a lawyer and give you the information before you decide you can disclose any of it. First of all, I have completed all transfer of money under your inheritance as Widow Goodson. The only thing left to do is the household liquidation in two weeks and then your inheritance will all be in funds, no property and other furnishings." Isaac took a moment to let his words register with Samantha.

"The advice I have is that your business should be kept private by you and as your lawyer, I am compelled to silence," Isaac said. "Another bit of business that will need to be done in Ohio Country is to have funds transferred there as soon as you decide on a couple of banks. They will be sought and notified when we get there to make the transactions. I suggest that you keep the auction money with you to use as needed. Do you have any questions?" Isaac asked.

"Why will I need a couple of banks when one would do?" Samantha asked.

Isaac pulled out a piece of paper. "This is a total dollar valuation for your private holdings. It is safer to put it in two banks," he said, "and it prevents one bank knowing your total assets, a strategy I believe to be more reliable for a woman."

Samantha's hand went to her mouth.

"Maybe you need your fan," Isaac said with a chuckle as he enjoyed the disclosure.

She fanned her hot cheeks. "I think I will keep it private. How will I need or use this much money?" Samantha said.

"You will get used to it and it is in safe keeping for you. You have no decisions to make with it until you want to use some. The next two weeks will be much too busy to do anything but work. The work for which you hired me is done. It will be separate work in Ohio Country to transfer funds. You can pay this bill when you receive proceeds from the auction," Isaac said and handed her his bill.

"Thank you. It will be a pleasure to pay you the money you have earned for an excellent job.," Samantha said.

"I do have a suggestion but you do not have to do it. You could sell the item instead but think about giving Percy the musket we found in the headboard trough of the bed since he has no gun to hunt with. He is ill-prepared for Ohio Country and hunting. He and Leroy could practice shooting at the farm if he gets it right away, but time is running out. The end of August is near?" Isaac said.

"That is a good idea, the gun for Uncle Percy. We should get it out for him. I do realize that August is closing fast and our lives will change. I am glad beyond words to express it," Samantha said.

Isaac's smile was evidence of his appreciation. "We can get the gun out this evening and he could start tomorrow," Isaac said. "We will have a short family meeting after supper if you agree."

"Yes I do agree and the women of the house have something to say," Samantha said.

"What would that be, Samantha?"

"You will find out tonight, Mr. Hogan," Samantha said. They both smiled.

Supper was short, more like a snack, and quick to clean up. Everyone knew they had a meeting to attend. While Catherine and Auntie Geneva put the kitchen in order, Samantha had Isaac go in the bedroom where the musket was still hidden. She remained timid about entry into the room and would never do so without someone with her. Isaac set the long gun upright with the stock on the floor and the barrel against the frame of the dining room door, just outside in the hallway. He had to hurry to get Little Margaret, who would not settle for anyone else since she knew he was present. He started the meeting while holding his adored daughter.

"We may all feel excited, as if a prize is almost reached, but we have two more weeks of hard work before we leave for Ohio Country," Isaac stated. Everyone's heads nodded in agreement. "A couple of things have been completed to make it all possible. They are the conclusion of Widow Goodson's matters and the sale of the house," Isaac said to sum it up. "We have the end of gardens to finish, food preservation nearly accomplished, and then the auction to be held. Oh yes, the loading of wagons on the last three days after the final sale. Have I missed anything?"

"I wonder if I will be getting the knife back from the sheriff," Samantha said.

"The knife is a subject I have asked the sheriff about again, since he has been noncommittal about an answer," Isaac said. "He is still vague, a sort of non-answer. I want permission to write a letter that you will need to sign with me. It will state a strong case that may get a swift compliance, which we desire. We can say that we are interested to know if the conditions at the jail have improved. We'll list the lack of fresh water for prisoners to drink and for washing, poor food, how the records for those items are itemized, finally, the possible disappearance of village money for such items. It could help to mention that the missionary society may be looking for a good cause. Does this sound like a letter you will agree with?" Isaac said.

When the knife conversation began, Percy sat with his head down and both hands brushing back against the sides of his hair.

Samantha laughed and enjoyed the smiles of approval from Catherine and Auntie Geneva. "I am completely on board with it and I think adding a deadline is reasonable since the end of August is near and time is running out for the return of the knife," she said.

"I will write it tomorrow and bring it at midday for your signature so it can be delivered immediately," Isaac said.

"Good," Samantha said. "Now, as you know, Isaac, the ladies have an important topic to cover. We need help with an urgent job and there is not enough time in each day to get everything done. We went to the cellar to find more wine but none is bottled at this point and we need to start bottling from barrels, since we must take what we can with us," she said. "The bottles should not be left behind and ought to be full to take with us so the space they take is not a waste. We could use help from anyone here who finishes work and would be available and willing to help with this job," she said.

Three men motioned with their hands.

"Leroy and I will be done with garden harvest within days," Percy said.

"My last official law job will soon be concluded," Isaac said.

Auntie Geneva, Samantha, Catherine, and Little Margaret clapped their hands.

"What exactly is the situation in the cellar?" Isaac asked.

"There are several containers of wine and we must bottle whatever is going with us. Any whole barrels left can be auctioned off," Samantha said.

"A 10-gallon cask of port wine weighs a good 90 pounds and will yield roughly that many quart bottles of wine," Isaac said.

"We can decide when to stop after one barrel is emptied but I think we will need at least two emptied and bottled," Samantha said. "We have clean bottles, since we washed them as we have used them. They will need only a quick rinse."

"The bottles will each need to be rinsed with a small amount of wine also, as the water for the first rinse will pollute the wine," Catherine said. "It has always been done that way. The wine used for rinse is then used for cooking so it is not wasted," she said.

Little Margaret thought her mother's words were reason enough for clapping and everyone joined her, to her delight. No one was immune to laughing.

"So, within days, the men are in a position to become wine bottlers. It leaves less time for Percy and Leroy to become familiar with an important tool that you have for them, Samantha," Isaac said. "Shall I bring it in, Widow Goodson?"

"Yes you may bring it in but you may also dispense with calling me that name, please," Samantha said.

"I do not believe you can dispense with it all together, Samantha. It can work to your advantage and all of us will need to use it when we think it is needed. Remember the lack of power when it was Miss Crow and try not to hate it," Isaac said. "You can easily explain widowhood without giving your privacy away."

"I know you are right but inside this house, calling me 'Widow Goodson' can be dispensed with, please," she said with her usual good nature.

Isaac stepped away to retrieve the Brown Bess Musket meant for Percy from behind the door frame. "Percy, this is from Samantha but she has something smaller to handle. You can use it out at the farm to practice until the three of us men need to get down to business with the wine bottles."

Percy stood up and gave a quick bow to Samantha. "Thank you, Miss S'manthy. I will need practice all right, never been allowed to have a gun, never," he said. "Thank you, Miss S'manthy. Thank you Mr. Isaac." Samantha loved hearing Uncle Percy say her name in his unique way.

"Percy, if you want some guidance on how to load and shoot, I can spare a little time early tomorrow," Isaac said.

"Yes, Sir, I could use a lesson to start," Percy said. He offered his handshake. Leroy wore one broad grin but didn't say a word. Auntie Geneva hugged Samantha.

"We will set up a target and practice range tomorrow at the farm for you and Leroy to use," Isaac said. "You will both be ready and able to hunt for game in Ohio Country to feed your family." The statements were fully accepted with everyone smiling. Leroy's smile was the biggest between him and his father.

"Samantha, Let me see your smaller gun?" Catherine said.

Samantha pulled her fan out of her left pocket. No one hid laughter as she put the fan back and brought the flintlock pistol out from her right pocket.

"Now that is pretty," Catherine exclaimed at sight of the silver filigree. "It is a ladies' pistol and you look the part, Samantha."

"I'd rather use the fan," Samantha said. They all laughed and the meeting was over.

Samantha read as late into the night as she felt was safe to do. She took notes to study the medical book and remember the difficult material, helping her retain significant details. She could recall information better for review after doing it that way.

She jumped slightly. What was that sound? Something in the side alley? Did an animal bump against the house?

Chapter 8

Night Watch
Late August 1783

Samantha awoke early and felt unease at the remembered sound she had heard in the alley during the late night before. She planned to mention it at breakfast and make sure they knew it was not her imagination. It played over and over in her mind, while she wondered who and what had happened out there at night?

Everyone was cheerful during breakfast and complimented Geneva on her cooking, which started the day well for all of them. Catherine offered to prepare food some morning so Auntie could sleep in.

"I have no desire to sleep in, Miss Catherine, and I manage to cook a breakfast easy enough while you work harder to take care of these little children," Auntie said.

"Samantha, you seem to have a lot on your mind this morning. What has you under its spell and looking so worried?" Isaac asked. They all looked at her for an answer.

"I was not letting anyone get away without a mention of what I have on my mind, but I wanted all of you to enjoy breakfast first," Samantha said.

"Don't hold back now. Just tell us," Catherine said.

"I did not sleep well last night after I heard a sound in the alley, a quiet bump against the house. My enjoyment of reading kept me up quite late. I continued to listen for someone out there, but whatever or whomever, they were stealthy and tried not to be heard. I fell into uneasy sleep, but I kept waking up though I heard nothing more. I don't think I will sleep at all tonight because it was not my imagination," Samantha said.

"We will take a look out there first of all," Isaac said.

Percy and Leroy followed Isaac outside.

Catherine was the worrier of the group. "We will certainly be glad when we leave this village," she said.

"We have done nothing to deserve poor treatment, not one of us," Auntie Geneva said.

"They have a guilty conscience over Cretia's death and would rather blame us for implied wrongs than admit they are wrong themselves, Auntie," Samantha said. "I hope it is better up north since rumor lends hope to that."

Auntie's eyes watered. She wiped tears away with her apron and said, "I heard the same, Miss S'manthy, and I pray it is true."

Catherine reached over and patted Auntie's arm. "I believe it is truer than not, Auntie because I have lived in the north, Pennsylvania to be exact. It's not close to perfect, but three-quarters of black people there live as free as whites and make a living with pay for jobs they do," Catherine said.

The men returned and Isaac spoke. "We see no unusual markings in the alley. The neighbors have a right to use it. Thing is, using it late at night when the whole village is asleep, whoever it was, can make you wonder if someone is up to no good after our recent experience. Percy and Leroy have discussed it with me and agreed that the three of us will take turns at night watch for our time left here," Isaac said.

Samantha heaved a sigh of relief. "I feel safer all ready," she said.

"I do, too, but I am sorry it seems to be necessary for our men to lose sleep. It is not even a danger for Percy, Leroy, and you, Auntie, but we need your help," Catherine said.

"We will all carry an equal load to get to Ohio Country," Percy said. "We need help, too, just to leave this place."

"That is the whole truth," Leroy said.

"Then it's settled. Now, you all go on out of here so I can clean my kitchen," Auntie said. She shooed the men out with a motion from her dish cloth. When the men were gone, she turned to Samantha and Catherine and said, "I will make sure my men-folk are awake at the proper time to come over for their watch."

"Oh goodness, that breaks up your sleep, too," Catherine said.

"We'll have to discuss it right after supper, how to handle it tonight, with who takes what shift," Samantha said. She started dishes and suggested that Auntie sit down and rest before more work began for the day.

"We are close to the end of harvest preservation. Only a couple more days of work remain and we can pack away all of the large canning pots and utensils into the waiting room," Auntie said.

"The men will be done before that and started on the draw off of wine from casks into bottles. And, by the way, Isaac has mentioned to me that both Leroy and Percy have managed to shoot with some good accuracy. He says it will help us all on our trip to Ohio Country," Catherine said.

"We are ahead of schedule and along with the accurate marksmanship, we're in good shape," Samantha said. Auntie was beaming.

~~*~~

The three women's food preservation was finished and they had stored it in equal allotments in the waiting room, ample food for each wagon. The same was done with the wine as the bottles were brought up. It was decided that more would be sold than carried north with them. One and a half wine barrels had been bottled and containers were in short supply after 145 quarts were filled. It left three untouched barrels full in the basement.

"They will fetch an excellent price, Samantha. They are too much weight to load on a wagon and take up space," Isaac said.

Samantha agreed.

The men took turns each night to stand guard and make sure that someone intent on mischief could do them no harm. Percy took the first watch. Leroy took second sentry when

Percy hurried to the cabin to rouse him. They insisted that Geneva would not have to wake up for their switch over.

"You just keep on with that good breakfast every morning," Percy said.

Isaac took the third look-out spot when Catherine roused him. She woke for baby Henry to be fed and that was sure to happen. Leroy went back to the cabin when Isaac took over. No mischief was done to them that they knew of and they wanted to keep it that way.

"We can only be sure of continued safety if we persist as night watchmen until the day we leave," Isaac said. They all agreed.

Isaac had the close of his office to attend to a couple of days before the start of the auction. Catherine had the care of her two children, which meant she was always busy.

Leroy had friends to see for the last time. Auntie was intent on thorough cleaning of the cabin they would leave behind. "The new doctor may have a use for it if he has help. We won't leave any mess behind to shame us," she said.

With the work caught up, Samantha decided she could afford the luxury of time to ride her horse. "I have missed riding and the feeling of freedom it gives me and Brown does need exercise," she said.

"I think I will keep watch while you give Brown a run," Percy said.

"Thank you, Uncle Percy. I won't be out there long really, since I can't go where I please on the road to the farm. I miss Brown and hope he also misses me," Samantha said.

Percy bridled Brown and led him over to the block Samantha used to gain height for mounting. "You spoil me, Uncle Percy. Usually, I have to do everything myself if I want to ride," Samantha said.

"It doesn't do any harm to give a hand while I can. We'll all pull our own weight when we need to during the trip," Percy said.

"I hope we don't have our locations split too far apart, Uncle Percy. I would enjoy having Auntie and you as my neighbor," Samantha said as she leaned down and hugged Brown's neck. He whinnied in a gentle tone and Samantha patted his neck. "Maybe I could hire you to help me out part time when we see what the situation is," she said.

"I believe we have to wait until we reach Ohio Country and see what the real situation is for all of us there," Percy said. "We can hope it will be possible and I know Geneva would like that, too."

Samantha nodded her head and knew it was sound advice. She let Brown take the lead and trot down the lane. Uncle Percy was still in sight when she turned around to gallop back. "One more time?" she asked. Percy nodded yes.

On her return, she slid off Brown's back and hugged him one more time. She smiled at the same familiar whinny. Percy removed the blanket that he had strapped on Brown and they rubbed him dry and turned him out to pasture. Samantha walked to the barn with Uncle Percy to put a bridle and blanket away. He stepped inside while Samantha waited in the shaded doorway. She looked over at the wagons lined up and hoped they would hold all that needed to be loaded to go on their trip north. It seemed to her that it could not possibly fit, but Isaac and Uncle Percy had said it would. She needed to trust their word and she did. Something had caught her eye before she turned to go.

"What is that under the wagon?" she asked Uncle Percy as he came out the door.

"Show me what you mean, Miss S'manthy," he said.

She walked closer to the nearest wagon with Percy right behind. Samantha did not have to show him what she meant. She heard his low whistle as he saw it, too. He was quick to bend under the wagon in an instant where he picked up a hand full of the sawdust mingled in the grass and weeds. He threw it down with disgust. Percy was instantly on his back looking up at the undercarriage of the wagon.

"Miss S'manthy, we have damage done," Percy said. He came out from under and went to check beneath the next wagon and found the same thing. After the third wagon, he came out and shook his head from side to side.

"Miss S'manthy, you were right when you said you heard trouble outside. We have two cuts sawed under two wagons. It would weaken them more by the time we get a couple hundred miles down the road. We'd be out there in nowhere and be hard put to repair them. We'll have plenty to talk about after supper. If Mr. Isaac comes back early before dark, I'll show him where 'snakes' left a sawdust trail in the grass." He shook his head from side to side in disbelief. "They are real sidewinders to do a thing like that, Miss S'manthy."

"I know it makes it dangerous for us, Uncle Percy," she said.

They walked toward the house. "I believe we better wait until after supper to let the others know, Miss S'manthy. No sense alarming them until they hear the whole discussion," Uncle Percy said.

"You are right, Uncle Percy. I have reading and studying to do and will keep myself busy so I won't be tempted to talk about this," Samantha said.

Isaac did come back early and Percy hurried him to the barn. They had time to talk it over before supper. After a small meal, it came time to inform Leroy, Auntie Geneva, and Catherine of the afternoon discovery from Samantha and Uncle Percy.

"We can be glad Samantha had good ears for the bump sound in the alley and also that she went for a ride on Brown today," Isaac spoke to the group around the table. "Tell them what you saw, Samantha, with Percy as your look out."

"I noticed some sawdust in the weeds under a wagon," Samantha said.

Catherine drew her breath in sharp enough for all to hear.

Isaac continued. "Percy showed me two wagons that were sawed underneath, not all the way through the reach of the under-carriage, but enough to weaken them and cause trouble. It could have caused injury if not noticed until on the trip north. Percy was quick to discover what the sawdust meant and he has the right idea about how we ought to restore them to a stronger condition. We will have just enough time to do repairs needed before loading our goods after the sale," he said.

"I will take a look first thing in the morning and I wonder why they sawed only two, "Leroy said.

"We talked that over, too. They hadn't finished before we started look-out and thwarted their plans. It turned out good when Miss S'manthy got nervous. Isaac and I believe they mean to cut the third one and it will not go unnoticed" Percy said. "We will be waiting on them."

Leroy chuckled. "I wouldn't want to be in the culprit's shoes," he said.

Catherine had not spoken yet and she looked worried. "Thank you, Samantha, for being alert. You have saved us a lot of trouble, especially since the wagons can be repaired before we leave. That much is a relief," she said.

"I'm thankful about noticing the sawdust, too," Samantha said.

"Now, we have a different situation where the barn has to be watched from both ends," Isaac said. "One man will sleep while the other two watch from just inside each end door. Then we rotate and another one will sleep. We'll need to catch up with sleep in the day time. It will require that we need one woman awake here in the house at night, on alert at all times." he said.

"There are three women here and we can all take turns," Auntie said.

"I want all three of us staying in the house. I would not want Auntie at the cabin alone and we need her," Samantha said. "But the one awake should have my hand pistol in her possession to signal with," she said.

"I agree, but only for signal use, as a last resort, if we need to come from the barn. I also feel the need to demonstrate the use of Samantha's flintlock, since there is no familiarity here with it." Isaac said.

Samantha pulled the handgun out of her pocket and handed it to him.

"This is a sensitive gun once you pull back this hammer into the cocked position. When it is pulled back, the flint is in a position to cause a spark the minute you fire it, or in plain words, pull the trigger. When you pull the trigger, the spark from the flint will ignite the gunpowder and it will propel the lead ball out of the barrel. Once it is fired, more gun powder and a small lead ball have to be loaded to be ready for the next firing. Is this clear enough, any questions?" Isaac said.

None came.

"We can keep the property and ourselves safe for the short time we have left in this village," Isaac said. Catherine sighed.

"We'll be just fine," Samantha said. "When you wake up to feed baby Henry, would you want to take the time right after that to stay on alert for us, Catherine?" Samantha said.

"Yes I will. It is the best time for me since I will already be awake," Catherine said.

"Which end of the night do you want to take, Auntie?" Samantha said.

"I believe I will do best to take first guard and then let Miss Catherine feed baby Henry before I lie down," Auntie Geneva said.

"I do like the early morning watch for me," Samantha said.

"It will be nice to hear the horses in their stalls," Leroy said as the night became dark.

"Before I forget," Isaac said, "I had a visit from a deputy sheriff today, Samantha. Your knife was returned." He presented it wrapped in newsprint.

"Our letter worked quite well," Samantha said. She was glad to have it returned to the set but could not help wondering where the small knife was though she never mentioned it out loud. She did not want to have a discussion about it.

The three men went to the barn as soon as full darkness descended enough to hope they would not be seen. They intended to let the one sleeping take a straw bed while the other two stood watch just inside.

The night contained no surprises.

The day was busy with the repairs on wagons. The men did not regain the lost sleep. Repairs were an all-day job and into half of the next day. When they were done, the men were confident that there would be no under-carriage breakage on the trip. They rechecked the third wagon again, but it was not in need of reinforcement.

Two nights before the day of the auction, Samantha sat in the dark in the early morning hours, wondering how the men on duty as barn sentries were doing. She smelled smoke and it seemed strange, out of place, since it was a hot August night, weather where no one had need of a fire for heat. Her breath drew in sharp and she felt hair stand on the back of her neck. Grandmother was in her mind telling her to trust her instincts.

Samantha flinched when she cocked the flintlock in the silence of the waiting room. She opened the side door of the dark room into the alley. Her slippers made no sound on the boardwalk. She left the door ajar to avoid the noise of shutting it. A moment was needed standing still in the darkness to adapt her eyes to the surroundings. She turned to face the barn in the distance to the rear and stepped silently a few feet to the end of the house. Now she knew where the smoke was coming from. A dark figure dropped the flaming wand he had used to set the back steps ablaze. He had seen her and ran away at the instant when Samantha pulled the trigger to fire her handgun.

Chapter 9

Glorious Auction Day
Near end of August 1783

The shot fired in the dark of early morning brought people out of their sleep. A small crowd gathered in the dim before dawn. The commotion brought the sheriff's deputy from the jail after a while. The identity of the arsonist was unknown as the junior sheriff wandered back to prisoner duty. The fire was out and the damage was confined to a few boards on the steps. No one offered to help Isaac, Percy, and Leroy put the fire out but they were astute spectators just like they had been on Cretia's hanging day.

Samantha watched the congeries and wanted to shout what cowards they were. But she knew she should not do it. She could not cry like Catherine did. Her anger was too hot. Auntie could not hug anyone until they went inside after daylight. Only then, she hugged

Samantha and told her she was brave and had saved them all. She hugged Catherine, too, and it made Catherine cry all the more.

"Miss Catherine, you have scared Little Margaret. Maybe you could teach her to be a brave girl," Auntie Geneva said.

Catherine stopped her sniffles after Auntie's gentle reminder. Baby Henry soon needed to be fed, and it put her in a better mood. Auntie Geneva held Little Margaret while she hummed and soothed them all. Samantha started breakfast and hugged Auntie's shoulders and said, "You just keep humming and it'll do us all good, Auntie. I have watched you cook many times and I must have learned something."

Isaac came in first. "Even in broad daylight we will watch the barn so nothing else happens. We need to come inside to eat one at a time if it can be arranged," he said.

"Of course, you can and it is ready now," Samantha said as she set a plate of pancakes in front of him.

"I could eat a bear," Isaac said.

"That is too bad since we only have pancakes and ham and eggs," Samantha said.

Isaac didn't seem to notice Samantha's attempt at humor. "Samantha, you need a better aim. The bullet missed the man who started the fire and nobody admits to having any idea who would have been out there trying to set the place aflame," Isaac said.

"It was accidental that I misjudged, of course. I believe I wounded him, but I guess he will not report it if he is only grazed. I have thought about it since it happened. If I had brought him down and maybe killed him, our plan to leave this place would be prevented," Samantha said. "The deputy sheriff would have been glad to put me behind bars if he found reason."

Isaac shook his head. "You have a point there, Samantha." He paused. "We would have quite a problem if we were held up from leaving after the sale conclusion." Almost as an after-thought, he added, "These are great pancakes, Auntie Geneva."

"Thank you," she said and smiled at Samantha.

Percy came in minutes after Isaac went out. Samantha set his plate in front of him and tried not to watch to see his reaction.

"Geneva, can you tell me why I'm being stared at out of the corner of someone's eyes?" Percy said.

Both Samantha and Auntie Geneva burst into laughter.

"You just eat without any more nonsense and hurry up so Leroy can take his turn to eat," Geneva said in her sternest voice.

"You don't fool me, Miss S'manthy," Percy said while looking straight at her. "You don't have to hit me with that pancake turner so I leave some of Geneva's pancakes behind for Leroy," Percy said.

"I won't hit you, Uncle Percy," Samantha promised. She could not stop smiling.

"Lord-a-mercy," Auntie said as soon as Percy closed the door.

Leroy arrived and was quick to eat and thanked his mother for a good breakfast. Samantha and Auntie were quite amused that no difference had been detected in the food. After Leroy had gone out the door, Auntie said, "You cook just fine, Miss S'manthy."

The day wore on with a few knocks on the door. Isaac was inside at the time and answered to the unexpected attention. He was overheard more than once replying, "I will convey your kind respect to Widow Goodson, who will be happy to know of congratulatory sentiments on her bravery." After the parlor door was closed, he had chuckled discreetly at the first message from a neighbor. "Widow Goodson, I believe this is what is known as respect for your actions," he said. "It appears that maybe some folks thought the fire was going too far against you this morning."

"It is nice to know but it is late to arrive. I could have used some open support while Cretia's trial was going on. Where were they then? Your family was threatened with danger, too, you know" Samantha said.

"Yes, they were. We'll repair the back steps before the day is over and be thankful it is only boards," Isaac said.

~~*~~

Samantha was happy when the household was stirring. The glorious auction day was here and they were so close to leaving this place, which had become a nightmare. Her early morning lookout duty ended at breakfast when the men came in one at a time to eat.

Auntie Geneva was up before daylight and making a fire to cook a hot breakfast. It was a day they had all waited for. They were anxious to start it, and especially to conclude it.

"We will not have a big dinner in the middle of this day, just bread and wine, so we must eat a hearty breakfast. You may as well eat first, Miss S'manthy," Auntie said.

"It sounds like a great plan. I may have an appetite as soon as I taste your wonderful food, Auntie, but right now I have none," Samantha said. "I just want the glorious auction to begin and end!"

"Glorious auction is a perfect way to put it, Miss S'manthy, and a grand way to start the day," Auntie said.

"I wish I did not need to be on hand here for the event. If I could have freedom, I would ride Brown to the farm and back," Samantha said. "Well, I'm dreaming. I must stay here."

"Freedom will come for all of us when we leave this place, Miss S'manthy. A sweeter time is almost here," Auntie said.

~~*~~

The auction ended at 5:00 p.m. sharp. "Can you believe the high prices that were bid by people to obtain the contents of this house?" Samantha said. "And we even have the use of the dining room table and chairs until the day we leave. Imagine that."

It seems like the effect of notoriety from the trial and your recent bravery are each to blame or maybe to credit for the bids," Isaac said.

"It feels like an apology from the village for all we have been put through," Samantha said. "I think I will donate the remaining books in the library to the missionary ladies. Those women would be good stewards to loan books out for others to read. Can you help me put that in action, Isaac?"

"I can and it would be a generous gesture to this town, at least to those who deserve it. If they accept the books, they will be coming in and out to get them while we load wagons," Isaac said.

"That is fine. I know Mrs. Carlton who signed the marriage certificate and is one of the missionary society ladies. The other women have seen me at church and will be happy to snoop in corners to satisfy curiosity while collecting books," Samantha said. "They will be able to gossip about it for months." She wrinkled her nose with a smile.

"Do I detect sarcasm, Samantha dear?" Catherine said. They both laughed.

~~*~~

The attention to watch the house and barn, including horses and mules, continued. No one was willing to let down their guard even with new attitudes in some areas of the village. The Hogan's wagon had been loaded the next day after the auction and pulled to the head of the wide alley.

Close vigilance went on.

Samantha's last possessions were handed upward and loaded in her wagon on the second day. There wasn't enough room for all of her belongings, which were packed tight. The third Conestoga for Percy and Geneva had more than enough room for Samantha's overflow of things along with more pots and pans. Before the auction, Samantha had insisted that Auntie take ownership of a few of the kitchen utensils since they were overly well stocked.

After early breakfast on their last morning, a few dishes and a griddle were packed and a mattress placed in each wagon atop the bed boxes as planned. Mattresses had been used on the floors for their last night in Goodson house. There were smiles in the kitchen as they ate two at a time, their guard down slightly. They would only be at complete ease after they were many miles away. "We will soon leave this place behind," Uncle Percy said. Samantha laughed out loud.

Chapter 10

Caravan of Three Wagons
September 1783

T he house had been handed over to Dr.
Manville with a polite thank you and
farewell. Samantha was careful not to
imply that she was grateful to have it off her
hands.

Everyone sat high in their wagon seats
while Percy and Samantha were last to climb
up into their wagon, ready to move out. Grant
Macon, their trail leader, spat a brown blob of
tobacco onto the ground and started off on his
horse while three wagons pulled slowly out
behind. At the edge of the village, Percy and
Geneva's community of neighbors fell in step to
walk beside the tall moving wheels and sang a
spiritual of freedom. They turned back when
they had sung their special good-bye.

Samantha could not hold back her tears.
Percy pulled out his handkerchief to blow his

nose. "I reckon Geneva and Leroy might be feelin' sentimental, too, but we are leaving of our own free will, nobody sellin' us off," Percy said.

"You will have your freedom on my word of honor, Uncle Percy," Samantha said.

Uncle Percy blew his nose hard.

They rode in silence for an hour or more and enjoyed the scenery. "Miss S'manthy, you can ride inside if the weather turns wet. Them clouds up there seem to be tellin' us somethin'," Uncle Percy said.

"Oh dear, how will the trailblazer find his way back if his trail marks are washed out?" Samantha said.

"Where do you see trail marks?" Percy asked. He wondered how he had missed them.

"There's one, a big brown blob," Samantha said, pointing to the evidence. Percy's laughter carried to all of the wagons, but there was no stopping to share the jocularity. The two rode along smiling.

It wasn't long before it started to rain, but the wagons continued in motion. Samantha climbed inside under the canvas stretched high overhead on the wooden hoops of the frame. She wanted to write in her journal every day of the trip north. She was determined to manage it by writing slow and deliberate inside the moving wagon.

Steady moving brought the caravan of three wagons out of the rain into sunshine. The plans discussed ahead of time called for travel an hour past the middle of the day before stopping to eat. There had been only one quick stop for necessity. They were a happy group when the wagons stopped in the shade under a grove of autumn ash trees. The evidence of previous campfires made large round overlapping circles of ashes, which had burned flat to the ground. They were long since cold, left by settlers who had camped before them. It was comforting to know that others had gone this way.

The three men, Isaac, Percy, and Leroy, started a fire. The large rocks left in place by previous settlers were ready to set a pot of stew on for heating. The three stones were spaced far enough apart to build a fire inside the center on the ground and a large iron pot would be supported by the granites, as it warmed. Auntie Geneva and Samantha filled the kettle with canned venison and vegetables, which they occasionally stirred. It needed heating through but no prolonged cooking. They smiled, knowing they had planned well.

While food heated, Little Margaret stood mesmerized beside the trail guide, Grant, as he played the banjo. When food was hot and bowls filled, the instrument was placed with his bedroll behind his saddle. Little Margaret clapped and no doubt expected adults to join her. They had their hands full and their appetites ready. Isaac fed his little daughter and when she could sit still no longer, he played with her while she ran around trees.

The horses had grazed and drank from a stream and were hooked back to the wagons. They had to be pulled across that same creek, but the wheels were broad width along with tall height. Their structural purpose was assurance that the water did not reach high enough to enter the bottoms of the wagons to spoil goods.

Samantha was ready to ride Brown until their next stop in the middle of the afternoon. She rode ahead and then behind, always keeping the wagons in sight. They were slow with their huge wooden wheels but sturdy for the conditions of the trails, which were little more than tracks the further they went. The wagons were headed northwest across Virginia. The day was long and everyone knew by evening that it surely would take most of the two weeks to arrive in Ohio Country.

The horses and mules had earned a night off to graze and rest. They were doing their job well. The men checked every hoof for any sign of trouble from loose shoes. Supper was wine and bread around a campfire for the evening when travel of the day was done. They toasted their first day out with success.

Little Margaret had pent-up energy after riding for hours and they clapped for her as she ran around. Every adult watched that she did not come too close to the fire. She was ready to stop the minute she saw the banjo brought out. Grant picked fast tunes to amaze her and then slowed them down. She was lulled to sleep and every one of them was ready to turn in.

One man would be on guard and then the next, but there were four of them so the loss of sleep was short for each one. The trailblazer said it was necessary because robbery could be avoided and threat of bears and mountain lions had to be eliminated. "All kinds of varmints out there," he said.

"We came from a village that had snakes and varmints," Isaac said. They all laughed. "We have put it behind us and should be able to handle anything out here," he said.

"I feel alleviated and happier, which I haven't felt for many months," Samantha said.

"We all have our own relief provided by this journey to Ohio Country," Isaac said.

"Amen to that," Percy said.

They climbed inside their wagons for their first night spent on the trail, except for Percy, who elected to take first lookout. He smiled when he hoisted his gun up to lie across both knees as he sat on the seat of his wagon. He would keep watch from a height, which seemed like a good vantage point. Leroy volunteered to take second sentry duty since Percy would have it easy to wake him up from inside their wagon. It was noticeable that they took pride in the trust given them with Percy's own gun.

Grant settled down by the fire with his bedroll and was used to keeping the fire burning. He spat his tobacco wad into the fire to be rid of it, but better yet to hear it sizzle. He said the fire kept wild animals away and saved his black powder. He had a supply of wood stacked and ready, which Leroy had helped carry into close range.

Samantha laid awake to think of her family and the future, which included her thoughts of Corporal Sutter. She may have slept a few hours when she woke to the sound of coyotes in the hills. It sounded like one lone coyote answered the serenade of the pack. She was glad to be inside a wagon under a quilt. She shuddered at the sound of howls but was glad to be in safe company with men on watch. She went back to sleep with Daniel Sutter in her dreams.

The next day and the next and several more were very much the same. Each day Percy set the rose cuttings out behind the wagon for the time they were stopped in the middle of the day. "They will get enough sunshine to keep the delicate new leaves alive, Miss S'manthy," he said as he made sure the stems were wet along with the dirt. "They should survive travel so we can have success."

They made steady progress with only small mishaps along the trail. There was the necessary greasing of wheels to be done with animal fat and on the seventh day, a wooden wheel spoke popped out. It had to be repaired so that the weak spot did not become worse. The men were equal to any task that came up.

Percy used a sharp flint stone to mark the wooden seat back at the end of each day of driving Samantha's wagon, which was his way to keep track of how many days they traveled. Samantha liked it and smiled with each scratch he made. "You are easy to please, Miss S'manthy," he said.

The longer Percy drove Samantha's wagon, the more he felt comfortable being himself and saying what came to mind. "Miss S'manthy, me and Geneva have some worry about what we will find for us folks once we get there. We won't be able to stake a claim, not even one acre. We didn't have militia duty to earn land for pay and we don't know what work will be available if there is any." He was worrying out loud. "We have always worked hard and we expect to keep at it but we will scramble to try to find work as the first action to take before we have a roof overhead," he said. He paused to catch his breath and think.

"The Conestoga will serve you for a while. I won't have a place of my own either, but it's not the same problem. I wonder if I can bring myself to live home again. It may be hard since I have been making my own decisions. I will be forced to decide how to handle my new freedom until my married life with Corporal Sutter begins. Now I don't even know when he will come to Ohio Country to find me but I know he will come. I worry terribly that we will miss connections again," Samantha said.

"We do pretty good worrying together, Miss S'manthy. Maybe we have to meet our situation when we come to it and know for sure what we are facing before we worry about what we ought to do," Percy said.

"That is reasonable, Uncle Percy. One thing for me is that I knew I would not stay in southern Virginia when my folks reside in Ohio Country. I want to see them even if I have to leave there with a new husband. I have no way of knowing if Daniel Sutter will stake a claim he is entitled to when he musters out of the army. He may have parents who need help in some other area. I just don't know, Uncle Percy, now that I think about it," Samantha said.

"Are you ready to go where he goes and let him be the boss?" Percy asked.

"I will manage to have a say and keep my own mind, Uncle Percy. I don't need a taskmaster and I could not be like Eunice Goodson. I will find a way to be in charge somewhat and it needs to be talked about before marriage so it is no surprise later on," Samantha said.

"I agree with that, Miss S'manthy, and I hope you will not meet with disappointment. If a man is seen by other men to be weak, he may be harsh with a wife to turn it around. Dr.

Goodson was extreme, but there are all kinds of in between," Percy said.

"There can't be many who are so evil as Dr. Goodson was, and I know Daniel Sutter is nothing like him," she said.

"It appears like we still wonder about the same things we were wondering about before we said it out loud," Percy said with a laugh.

"I guess we made no progress then," Samantha said with the same good nature.

The wagons were pulling into a grove of trees, but more wagons were there ahead of them. Grant was talking to another man with whom he shook hands when he rode up ahead of the lead wagon driven by Isaac. He finished his conversation and motioned for his wagons to pull in on the left of the ones already camped.

Percy pulled Samantha's wagon into the center between Isaac's wagon and Leroy's with his mother, Geneva. He had done it that way every evening so she would feel secure and it was especially appreciated from Samantha when other wagons with people were present.

After settling in, their fire burned down to red hot coals just right to heat a pot over, but they continued to gather wood for the night fire. They were ready to eat and had firewood stocked up for the night.

The families of both camps were friendly and sociable after all work and eating were finished. Grant Macon brought the trailblazer over from the other group and introduced him as Daniel Boone. He wore a coonskin hat with the coon tail hanging down the back.

Later, Grant told them, "Boone is already famous for trailblazing first with new trails, a pioneer ahead of us all. It earned him his title of captain in General Washington's Continental Army. Boone is on good terms with some of the Indians and it is good to stay in one caravan for both groups of wagons to pass through the next area up ahead. The natives respect Daniel Boone and he respects them. The Shawnees are peaceful people but have fought some settlers who infringed into their hunting grounds to settle in."

No one said a word while they listened to Grant explain Boone's reputation, which was refreshing and reassuring.

Samantha worried now about the thought of Indians and what could go wrong. She, Auntie Geneva, and Catherine talked about it among themselves. They were terrified because they had heard tales of scalping and it was fearsome to think of. Grant was able to soothe their worries by saying there had been no uprising in the area for many weeks and the Indians were at peace unless some group would treat them harsh and stir them up. Samantha and the women worried but felt some assurance because of several men in the two camps. They would do their best to get them all safely to the southern edge of the Ohio River intersection with the Scioto River.

Earlier Isaac brought up the subject about the military tracts in Ohio Country not being surveyed yet and being less accessible because of greater Indian danger to their families. It was discussed around the two campfires with all of the parties present and some settlers in the other camp were unaware of the information. Daniel Boone and Grant Macon upheld that it was true that the intersection of the rivers was to be one location for bigger camps while folks waited to go into Ohio Country. They were truthful men with the people they led when a question was asked.

It had been a restless night and Samantha suspected she hadn't been the only one lying awake into late hours and listening to sounds of the night. She thought of Corporal Sutter and knew she would feel safer if he were here with her. She wished for his presence and wondered how long she would be forced to wait to start a life with him. She knew she would wait for him and went to sleep with better thoughts than fear on her mind.

Morning seemed to come sooner than usual when sleep was so short that most of the camp had not slept well. They heard birds call and coyotes barking in the dark, and imagined they were signals from Indians. It caused fright when Indians were present as the wagons rounded a bend. They sat on horses in a group and Daniel Boone summoned Grant Macon to join him in greeting them. Together they rode up to the natives.

The caravan was stopped for what Grant later said, was a friendly visit and would benefit his next group of settlers. Finally, they were all moving and glad to turn more north than west. They had come to know that a change of direction would happen when they reached the Kentucky region, which was Virginia's territory on its western edge. They headed straight north toward the destination they had discussed in camp the night before. It was their tenth day and exciting to know that less than a few days stood between Samantha and a reunion with her family.

Chapter 11

Guilt and Confessions
September on the Trail 1783

At the midday stop for dinner, Daniel Boone and Grant Macon told their groups to be ready to move on as soon as they could. They would be pushing hard through the afternoon at a faster pace. Except for unforeseen obstacles, they would be within one day's reach of the Ohio Scioto River intersection by dusk where they would set up camp for the night.

"Isaac, what does this mean? I'm confused. I thought it would take 12 to 14 days to reach my family," Samantha said.

"It would have taken close to the 14 days if we were going into Ohio Country. Remember, it's to the intersection of the Ohio and Scioto rivers on the southern bank," Isaac said. "It is at least two days short of what it would take to cross over on the Ohio River ferry and travel up to Licking Springs, further north into the middle of Ohio Country."

"You mean that it is possible for me to see my parents tomorrow tonight?" she asked.

"Only if you are very lucky and that is not likely, so hold down your excitement," Grant offered in his blunt way when he broke in on the conversation. "We will camp tonight, and tomorrow morning we start a hard day of pushing all day to reach the Ohio River road.

Samantha was satisfied with plans for the next morning and the explanation of how it would unfold. She was glad that today they would push hard toward the Ohio River exactly north of them.

The night was too long for her excited state of expectation. Morning was never more welcome.

Her excitement was hard to contain as she rode in the wagon seat all morning. Uncle Percy seemed unusually quiet, perhaps ill-at-ease. Samantha wondered why.

She needed a change of scene.

Brown carried her through the first half of the afternoon until they made a necessary stop for everyone to walk and do whatever they needed for relief, including getting a drink.

Samantha, Auntie, and Catherine came back past a small hill with rocks on the slope. They had noticed them earlier and were mindful to use them as a landmark, so they wouldn't make a wrong turn. A young boy from a wagon in Boone's caravan climbed down the rocky slope and slipped on a rock as it dislodged and sent him for a tumble. The unexpected fall caused him to whoop as if he were in pain.

Samantha saw the real cause of his whoop just as a diamondback rattlesnake struck the back of the boy's leg. She pulled out her flintlock, cocked it, and shot the recoiled snake on pure reflex after the snake had lunged. The rattler in front of the fallen rock had been as startled as the boy.

"I need my medical bag and some wine, please," Samantha demanded in a voice louder than normal. Uncle Percy turned to go and get it. Samantha knelt on her knees beside the boy, who couldn't have been any older than her younger brother, Matthew. "Do not move yet," she cautioned the boy. She peeled off his deerskin boot and pushed his pant leg higher. She was not through demanding. "Flip over, face-down." He laid with his head uphill, the best position as Samantha knew and she was glad she didn't need to have him moved to keep the bite attack lower than his heart. Another push up of the pant leg exposed the imprint of a puncture, which was evidenced in the boy's tender calf. "You will lie still," she ordered. She bent toward the patient and spoke low, straight to the patient. "Good news, the strike missed on one side, just one puncture and a scrape there," she said. Her voice rose again, "Does someone have a raw potato I can use, please?"

Only half the venom entered his leg when one side of the fangs only side-swiped she told herself, and a better chance of recovery.

Samantha was aware of Uncle Percy's dark hand when he put the medical bag down within her reach. He leaned the wine on the grass slope. "Thank you," she said. She opened the bag and removed a roll of thin strip sheeting. She wrapped and tied it around the leg just above the hole made by the wicked tooth. She took the knife case out and then the medium size knife from its velvet mold. A small one would be a better choice for this task, but it was not available. It came to her mind, as it had in weeks past, pondering the whereabouts of the smallest knife. She didn't believe she would ever have the answer, and hadn't thought of it recently.

Uncle Percy slipped the smallest knife into the open case in front of her, placing it into its own velvet form. There was no pretense of hiding the fact that it had been in his possession. Samantha drew her breath in sharply, but there was no time for questions or explanations. They both knew they would talk about it. She continued with her first choice, the medium blade since the small tool must be cleaned before she could use it

"I will need two strong sticks for splints along both sides of the leg," Samantha said for anyone willing to act on cutting them. Percy moved to go, but Boone took the job.

Two men dropped down on either side of the boy. Each held an arm and a leg so he could not squirm away. They knew the boy, which was apparent when one man said, "You'll be fine, Asa," to reassure him. A potato rolled within reach near Samantha's bag. She heard a muffled cry coming from a female nearby but continued to cut above and below the lone puncture mark.

The patient had fainted with a slender piece of round wood branch between his teeth, which extended past both sides of his cheeks. It prevented biting his tongue. Samantha had a view of the back of his head. She sucked the venom and spat on the ground, repeating it again and again. She looked up and saw a woman being held onto by the other women from Boone's camp. She believed the woman to be the boy's mother.

"Thank you, Uncle Percy," she said as he handed her the wine with the seal of cloth, wax, and string already twisted off. She took several tastings, swishing each mouthful and spitting it onto the ground.

Samantha propped the wine against a rock and reached in her black bag for rolled sheeting. She remembered the old trick she had learned from Doc Murphy at the Yorktown camp where she had acted as nurse to help him during the last week of the decisive battle.

She cut two patches of cloth from the end of a long swath. One was used to wipe the blood from the wound. From a package in her bag, she placed tiny willow bark chips on the wound and several thin slices of potato on them. She applied a double square of cloth to complete the poultice. The wrapping was wound round and round the limb. More was needed for a red circle that widened and seeped through on the fabric both sides of the poultice.

She repeated the process with more sheeting several times around the leg and tied it fast. The splint sticks had been brought and the two men helped wrap the leg to secure them in place for immobilization.

Samantha understood the crying she heard from the boy's nervous mother kneeling beside him. She spoke to her quietly. "It will be best to have your son carried to the wagon and you will have to keep him off that leg. Have him sit up and be sure his heart is higher than his leg at all times. He will be sick and the leg will swell but he should recover just fine."

Samantha wiped the blade off on the grass and poured wine on it. She repeated it with the smaller knife and dried them to return both inside the case. She dreaded the compelled conversation that must follow when she and Uncle Percy would be riding along together again.

The mother, who someone introduced as Rhoda, thanked Samantha repeatedly. It was easier for Samantha to lend aid than it was to gracefully accept thanks. She shook her head yes but backed away with the medic bag in her hand. She leaned down and picked up the slightly used quart of wine and gave it to the woman. "Don't allow him to eat or drink until tomorrow but starting in the morning, this wine will help him for a couple of days as he recovers," she said.

Samantha stopped short when the dead snake dangled in front of her from the end of Boone's musket. "That, my friends, is what happens to a viper when encountered by a fearless hunter," he said. The small group laughed.

The snake was expertly skinned while a couple of camp boys watched Boone apply deft strokes of his knife. Grant supplied a long flat piece of wood to stretch the skin open and pin it fast for drying. It was a long snake that extended over and underneath and was pinned the full underside of the wood all the way to the end again. Boone handed the naked snake body to the closest boy, who dropped it on the ground with his reluctance to take it in his hand. The group was afforded another laugh.

Daniel Boone said, "This will make a meaty pot of soup. Is anyone claiming it?" No one did, but he stuffed it in a sack on his back and it seemed destined to become soup or bait.

Samantha left Brown tethered to the back of the wagon for the rest of the way as the caravan prepared to push hard for the afternoon. She had something special to write in her journal for the day, but first an unavoidable conversation must take place. There was no way around it. She feared disclosing anything about why and how the knife went missing. What would she say and where did Uncle Percy find it?

"Miss S'manthy, I know the willow bark placed on the boy's leg was to help the pain, but the potato slices, what are they for?" he asked.

"The starch in the potato draws fluid and it can remove more venom left after my effort," Samantha said.

Percy wasted no time in opening the conversation as he intended when he revealed the knife. "You seem to have a way of losing knives and by and by they return to you, Miss S'manthy. I've meant to talk to you about the puniest knife from the set. It is a relief to be honest about having it in my possession for a long time, since the day Dr. Goodson died, to be exact," he said.

Samantha's cheeks were hot, but her mouth was closed tight. She did not want this conversation. She wondered if she looked angry or scared, but she knew it was worry and guilt mixed together.

"I found the pointy dagger in the Sunday carriage that Dr. Goodson drove to church. It seemed accidently stuck there but couldn't have been there any more than a week because I had sharpened the whole set the week before. I placed it myself in the velvet mold of the box where it belonged at that time," Percy said. "It wedged between boards beside the foot box on the passenger side."

Samantha listened intently and knew Uncle Percy was right so far, but she believed the knife being found on the passenger side was telling of her guilt. The offer that it had been there no more than a week was no help to vindicate her feeling of guilt, in light of the location he had named for finding it. But somehow Uncle Percy hadn't tied its loss to precisely the same day that Dr. Goodson died, only that he found it that day.

She kept her silence since he had not asked her a question, and seemed to go on blaming himself for possession of it. She brushed a wisp of strawberry hair from her fiery cheek.

A bump in the road took Percy's attention with the team and wagon but when they were past the rough spot, he continued. "I knew I should bring it into the exam room but then the doctor's death left it forgotten where I had stuck it behind a beam in the barn. I even had a quick thought that I might be blamed with Cretia in the death if a knife was discovered in my possession. I was concerned more with Cretia's fate and didn't think more about the knife again until after the trial and we were waiting for the gallows with dread. I admit when I remembered it again, I considered keeping it because we were never allowed any type of knife for everyday use and certainly not for defense. It was against the rules of white owners to allow their blacks any weapon in case they would turn against a master. I never intended any harm, but a man wants to be treated like a man and act like one." He paused to catch his breath.

He started again. "The longer I had it after you were in control and treating us so well, Miss S'manthy, the worse I felt. I almost told you on the last day you rode Brown at Goodson House. I was all set to speak when I came out the barn door and that's when you noticed the sawdust under a wagon. It was the end of confession that day. It got put off because we all had that trouble to handle and you did not need more piled on."

Percy took a breath. "Then you went and gave me the musket and my guilt was a mile high. I want to start with complete truth in

Ohio Country and I hope you can accept that as the whole truth and let me redeem myself in some way when you may need help in the new territory. I wanted to tell you in the beginning days of this trip, but it would not come out of my mouth," he said.

Percy's eyes looked straight ahead, watching the trail as he drove. He was finished with his confession and suffering from the ordeal of telling.

Samantha knew she was not alone in her guilt and was relieved after what Uncle Percy had revealed. Now she needed to confess her own guilt and maybe he would feel better. It was no time to hold back when Uncle Percy had opened a flood of words to reveal his truth.

"Thank you, Uncle Percy. I have something to say, too, and I have some guilt here. I took the delicate knife from the case to begin with. I had removed it the night before Cretia stabbed Dr. Goodson with the medium size knife. If the smallest one had still been there, maybe she would have chosen it. Maybe it would mean he would not be dead from a shorter point. I know Cretia thought that precisely because she mentioned it to me in her cell that the littlest knife was missing and she had to use the next biggest one. I didn't admit anything to her about me having it and maybe thinking of using it like she did with the one she took. Like you, I wondered right then if I would be charged for my intention even though I did not get to use it. If I had been under suspicion, I might not have been allowed to help Cretia in court to tell about the evil doctor. I wondered if implicating myself would make me seem guilty and my word untrue about what happened. I have felt guilt over not speaking up and the longer time dragged on, the harder it is to speak of it. I don't know even now if I would have used the blade, but I reached into my dress pocket to get it when Dr. Goodson forced me inside and down the hallway. The knife was gone after falling through a hole that the sharp point cut in my dress pocket."

She had to pause but caught her breath and started again.

"There was such a noise between me pleading with Dr. Goodson to stop that nothing else was heard, not even Cretia coughing, if she did. I had no idea she was present inside that room, nor did he, it seems. When I was well enough to go to the jail to visit Cretia, I first took the time to look for the knife near the boardwalk in front of Goodson house. I have worried many times about where the knife was and I never once mentioned it to my lawyer, Isaac, either.

Later when I was well again after the ordeal, it became necessary to mend the pocket and that caused me to have more guilt. You don't owe me any restitution because we seem to be even in our guilt. Can you forgive me my silence, too, Uncle Percy?" She burst into tears and was done talking.

When she was composed again, she looked at Uncle Percy. He made use of his handkerchief to blow his nose. His tears were as real as Samantha's. "We both had our mixed-up reasons and we can start fresh and honest with our new life ahead," he said. "I feel better, Miss S'manthy."

"I do as well, Uncle Percy," she said.

They both began to smile and Uncle Percy laughed out loud.

Chapter 12

Ohio Scioto Camps and Cabins
Destination, September 1783

Samantha climbed into the interior of the wagon. She finished her journal entry by writing that her own knees had seemed as weak as those of the mother, Rhoda, only after the snake ordeal for the boy, Asa, had been concluded.

She reloaded her gun with black powder and was ready if it was needed again. She marveled at how she had grown used to having it and did not want to be without it now, since it had proved to be so valuable to her. She wondered, what her parents and Corporal Sutter would think of her handgun? When would she feel comfortable to tell Mother she had it? She was expected to use a musket and had practiced with Jonathan, but this flintlock was not in their realm of experience. It was in hers and she liked it.

Samantha smiled as she took care to wrap the black powder supply away and was cautious not to spill one bit on her navy and gold dress. The folds of velvet hid her pocket where the flintlock was held in readiness. She leaned back to think and rest.

Samantha was amazed to wake up and know that she had fallen asleep and had so far missed the sights of the afternoon travel. She'd had no intention of missing anything. She started to climb into the front seat of the wagon, but the stretched snake skin on the board had fallen across her usual seat. She pulled it into the interior and took her seat opposite Uncle Percy as he drove the team.

"What will you make with that long snake skin, Samantha?" Uncle Percy asked.

"I will have to think about it while it has lots of time to dry," Samantha said.

"You are the talk of the day with your decisive action to save that boy. Did you surprise yourself, too?" Percy asked.

"I did surprise myself but not at the time I had to act. It was afterward that I was surprised at how well I remembered reading the steps to be taken after a snake bite. I tried to memorize it by reading it over, making notes, and planting it in my mind before going on to something else. I am so glad to have the medical manuals to study," Samantha said.

"I am proud to know you, Miss S'manthy," Percy said.

"We both feel the same toward one another, Uncle Percy," she said. Their smiles remained, now more than ever.

The trail was well-trampled at the section they were in and the air was heavier after it had rained. The dust hovered only a few inches off the damp ground in spite of the many churning wheels of the wagons ahead of them. Samantha sensed excitement in the air and imagined that they would come into sight of her parents at any moment.

It was dusk when they circled the wagons for night camp. They were not alone in the area. Many groups of wagons were present. One circle consisted of 12 wagons all facing into the circle with one large fire in the center. They were a loud bunch and seemed to own the place. Grant informed them that some groups of people had been there longer and were well-acquainted with more neighbors so they could form a cohesive group.

Squawking birds were noticed circling and gliding overhead. Word from around the camp named them as seagulls looking for scraps of food. Samantha had no doubt of what they were since they had been prevalent at Yorktown on Chesapeake Bay.

"Maybe we should throw some raw snake to satisfy them," Percy said,

"You should never lose your sense of humor, Percy," Isaac said, apparently amused.

"The gulls mean that we are close to the water," Catherine said. Little Margaret was not sure she liked the large birds that swooped close and other times ran fast across the ground toward her looking for food scraps. She dropped a piece of her biscuit and several gulls fought over it, one grabbing it just to have another one grab half the prize away. Margaret had to be saved by her father who soothed her and promised they would not get her. She was happy to cling to him.

Catherine reminded them that the bread loaves had been depleted and no more would be available until they had a way to bake it. Auntie Geneva had baked an extra supply for the trip and it had served them all. Now they would miss having it.

Grant had a few words with his group around their campfire.

"Early in the morning I will ride out to search for the exact location of the Crow family. There are many families camped along the banks of the river." He turned to Samantha. "Your family is hidden among the camps somewhere and I will find them," he said.

"They live in a cabin very near the intersection of the rivers," Samantha said.

"That could make it easier to find them, but there are many dozens of cabins and tents with clusters of covered wagons to look through. I will be up early tomorrow to go scout for them and come back to camp for breakfast before we take the wagons out. When we travel tomorrow, it will be on a direct trip to their location. Boone will decide the direction for his company and we part ways when we move out after breakfast," Grant said.

It seemed like a letdown to have to settle in for the night after the excitement of the day. Tonight really would not be the time for finding Samantha's family.

As she lay awake thinking, Samantha wondered about details of any difficulty in being home again but longed to be there. She didn't want to clash with Mother and would have to be careful. She had endured hardships they knew nothing about and had grown past the girl she was when her family left the farm. Would they see that she was a woman now like they had said they expected of her? It was up to her to introduce the new Samantha, and she planned to right away.

Morning came the same as any other day, but it was a new day for Samantha, a hopeful day, which meant her life was changing again. Auntie Geneva and Catherine looked at her with a sweet expectancy because it was to be her day to have her family again after so long a time spiced with hardships. Their happiness for her was genuine.

They were all pleased to share in a breakfast that included a plump loaf of bread that had been brought to Samantha by Grant Macon before they had gone to sleep the night before. He had delivered it from Boone's camp, given by the mother of the boy who had been snake-bitten. It represented a grateful gesture that Rhoda had sent to Samantha. Her cheeks had reddened while standing by the campfire, but the night and the flickering flames concealed her rosy complexion.

The wagons were ready to move and Grant rode out front in his usual way as a guide. Samantha watched everything unfold as they were on their way past camp after camp. She saw rough shacks and wondered if any of them would be the place and was glad when they passed by. The Ohio River came into sight past the trees as they heard its lapping waters on their right. The small caravan moved west along the river road, which was settled in with all manner of cabins, shacks, and tents. There were wagons everywhere and the animals that pulled them, from horses and mules to oxen. There were no breaks in settlements as the population teamed with activity. There were pastures for animals to subsist on in between the variety of homes

Samantha looked for a clue to finding the first glimpse of her family. She found it in a field when she saw the two ordinary work horses, Jim and Babe, from the former Crow farm. Uncle Percy knew she had seen something familiar when she sat on the edge of the seat and couldn't take her eyes off those horses. They turned left into a dirt road running down the length of the fenced pasture and she saw a cabin come into view. It was ragged but solid and she strained to see who was standing on the steps. It was Matthew, and he was bigger than she could have guessed he would be.

Her excitement mounted and she reached back behind her for the sack of baked honey rolls she had saved for her younger siblings. She had four rolls to give them each a wrapped sweet and didn't want to forget them in her haste to see every family member.

Matthew watched the wagons with interest as they came closer. In his characteristic way, he opened the door to his home and called inside to the family that somebody was coming. Samantha remembered when he did that another time when she, Jonathan, and Father had come home from the battle at Yorktown. This time they should expect her arrival if they had a letter she had sent and because Grant had located them before breakfast.

She did not expect to see Grandmother. She was too well aware that there had been a death in her family in the middle of May and this was the middle of September, four months later. It would be bittersweet to see her family with her loving grandmother missing.

Percy pulled to a stop past the gate so she could walk behind it to go into the yard. She was aware of the two other wagons still moving down the dirt road but had no patience to wait for them to arrive. She dismounted her side of the wagon and arrived at the gate where Uncle Percy, wearing his broad grin, swung it open for her. She and Matthew reached each other and hugged soundly. He was smiling as she handed him the bag of sweet rolls, saying they were for him and their little sisters. Samantha went up the steps with Matthew following behind. Father opened the door and pulled her in, making it seem like he had waited for this moment that she would come home. He had sadness about him she could not remember seeing before, but he was glad to see her. "Your mother needs you, Samantha," he said quietly.

She looked toward the back door that opened and Mother came in with an armload of clean clothes off the clothesline. She left the door ajar and laid the clothes in a chair to have arms free to embrace Samantha. Mother found it hard to kiss Samantha's forehead and said, "You have reached your adult height." Mother's eyes were moist and Samantha missed her dear grandmother at that moment more than ever.

Her three little sisters came in the door Mother had left open for them and were so shy they could hardly look at Samantha. Matthew handed them the treat that they were not too bashful to take from him as he explained that their big sister had brought it. Samantha was surprised with the girl's growth and how pretty they were.

She could wait no longer and had to ask, "When will Jonathan be home?" She was anxious to see him.

It smelled like Grandmother's roses and thyme in the room and was a sad reminder of her. It was at the same time that Grandmother came in the door with a basket of clothes. Mother's forehead wrinkled as she put her hand to it, signaling a headache as tears filled her eyes. Samantha froze for an instant and felt the color drain from her face. She allowed Mother's hug, while knowing that something was very wrong. Grandmother's arms circled them both and Father cleared his throat and embraced them all. Grandmother had to sit down and she rocked in her chair while Father managed to say that Jonathan had died on the train track in an accident, as the night watchman.

He said nothing more and Mother couldn't speak. Samantha could neither speak nor cry as the shock left her stunned. She thought of the tree house back at the Crow farm, a place to run to, and realized she would not have run to it now even if it were close enough. She would face this heartbreak with her family, but it was too new to comprehend the impact all at once. Her thoughts were in slow motion.

Mother composed herself enough to say, "It is hurtful for you, Samantha, but it is not the same for anyone who has never been married nor lost a child, especially their firstborn." Samantha felt herself stiffen, but she held back any answer she could have given until she could give a softer reply than what Mother's harsh words had stirred in her. It was long seconds before she said, "I am sorry for your pain, Mother, and for yours, Father," as she turned to him. She saw Matthew with the sweet roll still wrapped and held in his hand, uneaten. He backed away with pain on his face and escaped to his room. Samantha followed and sat on the edge of his bed and cried with him, her arms around his shoulders and her wet face buried in his back as he sobbed into his pillow. She managed to stop crying and sat up. "I love you, little brother," she said. She walked out and closed his door to let him recover in his own way.

She hugged her grandmother and mother again. "It is painful to lose Jonathan and I will never forget him," she said through tears. She cried because she had too and her family cried with her. When she was spent, she sat in shocked silence. Her mind replayed the same unending thought: Jonathan is gone. Jonathan is gone. My dear brother is gone, and I will never see him again.

It occurred to Samantha that she hadn't asked or been told exactly what had happened to her brother on the train track. "What happened? How did he die?" she asked.

Father cleared his throat and said, "We will need to walk outside and I may tell you, but it is hard to speak of and just as hard to hear." He took her arm and started in the direction of the door.

A knock on the door startled everyone. Samantha jumped. "I forgot I had friends waiting outside," she said. She opened the door and Isaac stood there.

"I'm so sorry, Isaac," she said.

"Can we park our wagons and camp out in the backyard by the clotheslines for a night or so to get our bearings?" he said.

Father came to the rescue and said, "Yes, of course. Let me help direct you into place." He went out with Samantha right behind him. At the bottom of the few steps, Samantha introduced Isaac as her good friend and lawyer.

"You said he is your lawyer?" Father asked.

"Yes, Father, he is my agent and a close friend," she said

"You had need for council, you say, that right, Samantha?" Father said it with a sense of disbelief. "I cannot imagine why you would have needed hired direction."

"I will explain, Father, but we must get the wagons parked. Isaac's wife and children and our mutual friends are also here," Samantha said.

"Samantha, perhaps we should not be a bother," Isaac said.

"You are not a problem, and I can explain later what happened that I did not come right back out," she said.

"Friends of Samantha's are no burden," William Crow said. "We'll have you pulled right in and we'll see what can be found to eat."

"We had a big breakfast just over an hour ago," Isaac said. "Thank you but we could not eat more after plentiful campfire food."

Samantha was grateful for Father's hospitality and introduced him to Isaac's family along with Percy, Geneva, and Leroy before the wagons were parked.

"These animals can be turned into the field in the front if we can lead them around there," William said to Isaac. The four men started the process of removing harnesses and taking the mules and horses to pasture.

Samantha took Catherine and the children and Auntie Geneva inside to introduce them to her mother and grandmother, who had mostly recovered from telling Samantha about her brother. Samantha wanted to tell Catherine and Auntie, but it remained unspoken. She was a grown-up and she would not speak of it until it could be told privately. She had to wait. She could not say it to them until she could believe it herself. It revolved in her head. Jonathan is gone. Jonathan is gone. No. Please no.

Samantha's three youngest siblings were happy to play with Little Margaret and not bashful at all with a child. She was like a real live doll to them and Margaret loved the attention. The girls shared their dolls with Margaret, who kissed them all.

"Samantha, when will we meet your brother, Jonathan, whom we have heard so much about?" Catherine asked.

Samantha broke into sobs she could not control. Mother managed to say there had been a terrible accident and Jonathan had died. "William will tell Samantha the details later," Mother said.

"We don't need to hear about it until Samantha knows herself. We are so very sorry for the sorrow of your whole family," Catherine said and Auntie Geneva agreed.

William Crow had explained the situation to Isaac, Percy, and Leroy as they worked. All of them were somber as they came in. It was clear that each one knew of the sadness. Later, Isaac and Percy would tell their families how Jonathan had died.

Chapter 13

New Understanding
More Waiting, September 1783

Samantha pulled the paper out of the double-heart pocket of her apron. The words written by Daniel Sutter were worn and faded on the note. They did not pull at her numb heart strings in the midst of despair over Jonathan. She wanted to try, for Grandmother's sake, to make herself think of something happier than the loss of her dear brother. She often did not hear what was being said to her and conversations in the room went over her head while her thoughts replayed her disbelief. Jonathan can't be gone. He can't be gone.

Mother gave her the present saved for her that had been made by her brother. She held it against her wounded heart, a wooden jewelry box with double-hearts on the lid. It matched the trunk she owned with the same dual-heart design with leather strips for hinges. The hearts were her own special message from Jonathan. Of the two especial loves she had, one was in the grave and the other was not within her reach. She looked at the words on the note lying in her open palm and wondered if she could love Corporal Sutter if he arrived and didn't think she could anytime soon. She didn't believe she could get over her brother's death. She pushed Daniel's message away, closing it in the jewelry box where she discovered the knife she had given to Jonathan. Mother had mentioned that it was inside. It was something he had touched. How could Jonathan be gone, how could he?

Mother spoke to Samantha, but she stared straight ahead without hearing or seeing anyone present. She had no appetite and Marilla wanted her to eat. She would feel better herself if Samantha could eat.

"Dear, let me take you for a walk," Grandmother said. Samantha was pulled up but not away from her sad thoughts as she followed where Grandmother led her out the door and into the backyard. Grandmother walked with one arm around Samantha's waist. She was older and bent but Samantha's arm lay lightly across Gram's shoulder. Samantha didn't talk and Grandmother seemed to know it was not required and it could wait.

Auntie Geneva walked her outside the next day and hummed a spiritual as she slowly walked. Samantha didn't talk, but Auntie did. "Miss S'manthy, this is another hurt too deep to take on but we don't always have a choice. Someday soon you will feel better for a little while and another day after that you will feel better for a longer while. We have to live even when we think we can't go on and time goes by and we start to feel better. God knows we can't carry the heaviest load every day so he helps us recover a little bit at a time. You will see, Miss S'manthy, you will see," she said. Samantha burst into tears and Auntie held her and cried with her. She was afraid depression was deepening and knew everyone shared the same worry for their dear girl. Auntie held her and rocked her where they stood. "My dear girl," she said aloud.

Samantha could think about her family long enough to see that they ate, they slept, and occasionally they laughed and her friends did, too. How did they do it? She could not concentrate on them because they were fine, just fine. But she wasn't fine and she didn't know how to accept that her dear brother was gone. Jonathan please don't be gone. Jonathan, please. I came home counting on my brother who loved me best and you can't be gone. I need you here, Jonathan. I can't bear it without you. Her mind pleaded with Jonathan over and over.

On the fourth day, Father was more worried about Samantha. He had thought she would pull out of it, but she hadn't. He was glad he hadn't added more details on how Jonathan had died, cut in two by the train wheels that way, his foot held fast under a rail and his body dragged, mangled. Maybe it was time to take her up the hill to the grave. He didn't like indecision, but this was delicate to handle and he didn't want to harm her. He thought about it and waited until they had the midday meal.

"Samantha, you need to eat something to have the strength to walk to Jonathan's grave with me. I planned to go right after dinner if you are up to it," he said.

Samantha looked up at Father, trying to register his words.

Auntie Geneva was quick to grasp what William Crow was trying to do. She set a plate of food in front of Samantha and watched from her vantage point by the stove. She had insisted on doing equal work with Marilla Crow whom she had come to count on as a friend. Catherine tried to help, but she had the two smallest children to care for. The three women were equally concerned about Samantha's extreme reaction to Jonathan's death and were watching to see if William would be successful with trying to bring her out of it.

"His grave? Where is his grave, Father?" Samantha asked.

"I'll take you there when we have both eaten," he said, "just you and me."

Samantha picked up her fork and ate methodically until half the plate was empty. Auntie was humming and Marilla was smiling. Father was waiting. He stood up when Samantha laid down her fork. Mother wrapped her own shawl around Samantha's shoulders. Samantha sensed her presence and pulled away.

Geneva put her arm around Marilla's waist and they leaned against each other.

Father stepped out the door with Samantha on his arm. He positioned his hat on his head and they walked slowly up the hill. "I am sure you do remember going to the grave of a slave with me, too," Father said. "You and I seem to feel these things deeply, the importance of graves."

"Yes, Father, and I went to the slave's graveyard at Mt. Vernon to see the stone that was carved for Gowdy Lee," she said.

"We have to honor those gone too soon by caring for their graves the best we can," he said. They walked slowly and turned toward a gnarled old tree off to the left of the dirt wagon path at the top of the knoll. When they reached it, Samantha saw the simple wooden cross with a blue bow tied to it and some wilted flowers lying on the ground before it. There was no name on it and it bothered Samantha.

She caught her breath to speak. "Father, we must have a stone carved for Jonathan's grave, we must."

"I wish I could, Samantha, but I have the responsibility of several mouths to feed and they are first," he said earnestly.

"Please let me be the one responsible for it, Father. I can pay for it. I will look into having it made right away if you think Mother won't mind."

"I believe you should talk with her about it, Samantha, and she will probably be glad if you can do it. You had better check on prices as they may be far too much, especially having it engraved," he said.

"I will have Isaac find out where the stone can be bought and carved. He is great with details. I want to look at stones right away and pick one out. Do you think Matthew would want to help me with that?" she said.

"Yes, yes he may, Samantha. He is having a hard time and you might be the one to encourage him to pull out of it. Even if it proves to be too expensive, Matthew will benefit from helping uncover the details," Father said. "We can all help each other. Mother should be asked to contribute a few words to carve on it."

"I'll try to be better, but I loved Jonathan more than Mother thinks. It is hurtful for me that she dismisses my feelings for Jonathan as being less than hers," Samantha said.

"She means well, Samantha. I am sure she thought she was helping you. She doesn't want you to hurt because she loves you," he said.

"Father, I have hurt more than you or Mother could know. I need to tell you what happened so you will understand me better when I need...when I...Father, we have to talk soon."

"What is it, Samantha?"

"I need my independence understood and I need to talk with this family about events that happened to change me. All of my friends know the details and it is why I needed a lawyer. I am willing to let Mother and Grandmother read my journal and I have the newspaper accounts of what happened. I always planned to share the information so you could know what took place. Mother deserves to be told so she can understand. Maybe you are right that she meant well, Father."

"We can plan on a family meeting after all of the children are tucked into bed, if that sits well with you," Father said.

"Yes it does, Father. Thank you."

"I had held onto the knife you gave to Jonathan, the one that belonged to the slave before you got it, the one General Washington gave to you to keep," Father said. It was placed inside the jewelry box Jonathan made for you."

"Yes, Father. It was as Mother said I would find inside. Thank you for holding it for me. I want to give it to Auntie Geneva since I received it from the slave, Gowdy Lee, who was her brother. To be fair, I think she will be the proper one to decide what is to be done with it," Samantha said. "I am pleased to be able to give it to her."

"He was her brother? I believe, you must know, of course. Maybe you can give it to her at the meeting," he said.

They walked down the hill with a faster step than before. Father held onto the hand on his arm and was grateful.

It was clear to everyone that Samantha had turned a corner and she was coping better with her sorrow. William smiled at the circle of family and friends surrounding the table when he told them that a meeting would be held after supper.

Matthew had missed the announcement and Samantha was happy to see him in the backyard where he was sitting on a stump to whittle. "Little brother, we will have a family meeting this evening, just so you know," Samantha said. She had smiled at him and was pleased with his smile in return. She jumped down from her wagon where she had gone to pull out her journal and news clippings to share for the meeting.

"Matthew, I will need some special help soon and Father agrees that I can get you to help if you are willing. I am planning to pick out a gravestone and have it carved to mark

Jonathan's grave. Will you help me with that job from start to finish?"

"You want me to help? When will we start?" Matthew said.

"We can get Isaac to find where stones are sold and engraved and then we will have to go and look at them together. It will be mentioned at the meeting about the two of us doing this project," she said. Samantha had all of his attention and his smile was spreading

Supper was finished. Grandmother and Catherine had tucked children in their beds where prayers were lovingly heard. Samantha noticed the regular routine and was comforted by it.

The table had no elbow room left with so many gathered around. Grandmother preferred her rocker. Samantha dried the last dish and went to take a seat beside Mother. On an impulse, she put her arm around Mother's shoulder and kissed her forehead before she sat down. Father cleared his throat and Samantha understood at that moment that he fell back on his old habit, often when emotions intervened.

Father cleared his throat yet again and continued. "I believe the first order of business will be to talk about Samantha's request that she and Matthew will locate a gravestone marker and determine if one can be afforded for Jonathan's grave. Is anyone opposed to turning the project over to Jonathan's two oldest siblings?" he asked.

No one raised an objection to deny them the privilege. "We look forward to what you and Matthew will come up with," Father said, looking at Samantha.

He chose a new subject. "I am not asking for discussion on this idea right now but I suggest that we all start thinking about the winter coming and the wagons not being warm enough for sleeping as they are now. We need to come up with solutions soon and will discuss possibilities next meeting."

He cleared his throat and began again. "We have a topic or perhaps two that are important to Samantha and she will let us know what they are," Father said.

"Thank you, Father," Samantha said. She opened the jewelry box and pulled out the knife that had belonged to Jonathan. "The return of this knife to me is unexpected since I gave it to Jonathan," she said. "Before that it was given to me by General Washington. I obtained it from Gowdy Lee, I am sorry to say, because of the circumstance."

She paused as Auntie gasped and Percy and Leroy each put a hand on Geneva's arms to steady her. "I want you to have it, Auntie, and you should do whatever you think best with it, since we know it is more rightfully yours than mine." She slid the knife carefully across the table to Auntie. "It used to have a holster, which seems to be missing now," she said.

William Crow did not explain the loss of the holster, though he knew it had been ripped away during Jonathan's accident.

Father spoke. "I continue the yield of the meeting over to Samantha. She has information that she feels her family should know and she believes her friends can give credible help to her by upholding her telling of the information. Begin when you are ready, Samantha."

"I'm ready. I've given it enough thought. I am not the same innocent girl who stayed behind to wait for Corporal Sutter. I also need to say that I don't blame anyone here for problems that befell me when my family left the farm and I stayed behind to work for Dr. Goodson. I wanted to stay and I learned a lot of skills when Dr. Goodson was acting like the man you thought he was, Father. I am a midwife and a healer because of those skills and my further independent studies of medical manuals. None of us had any idea that Edgar Goodson had an evil side, which overran any good he did as a doctor. That is the side that was hidden from everyone except Eunice Goodson, who he often beat, Cretia, who he raped, and me who he also raped and forced into marriage. We came to the point of wishing him dead," Samantha said.

Mother had gasped more than once and Samantha stood silent for a long moment and waited while the information sunk in.

"I believe Auntie Geneva wished him dead, too," she continued.

"Yes, Miss S'manthy, I did," Auntie said.

"I miscarried during another beating. Poor sick Cretia killed Dr. Goodson to stop the abuse and the beatings," she said.

Mother was sobbing and wiping her face with her apron hem. Father reached over to steady Marilla and cleared his throat. He excused himself to blow his nose. Samantha stood silent. She had her mindset to control her emotions in order to finish speaking about what had happened and why she was not the same girl they had left behind. She took a deep breath and stood erect, waiting.

Grandmother's eyes were closed, but it did not stop tears as she rocked. Matthew's mouth had dropped and his eyes were on Samantha's face. Father sat back down and cleared his throat. He silently shook his head.

"The newspaper clippings tell that Cretia hanged for the murder, but she was nearly dead from the same illness of consumption that Eunice died from. We had no idea Cretia planned his death, but no one is sorry he is gone, only that Cretia suffered and died. She gave her last breath and strength to set me and her family free," Samantha said as she swept her arm toward Auntie and Uncle Percy.

"Yes, she did, Miss S'manthy," Auntie said. Percy and Leroy nodded in agreement.

"Let me also speak for Samantha," Isaac said. "I presided over the trial for Cretia and all of us accompanying Samantha now were there to witness what took place. Samantha testified and paid for Cretia's defense. Cretia had every care that her good friend could give," he said.

Grandmother left her rocking chair and reached for Samantha to hug her. "I love you, Dear," she said. She picked up a newspaper clipping on top of Samantha's collection and was standing between William and Marilla to share it with them.

Samantha had told it as plainly as she could and would answer any questions they had. She heard them say many times how sorry they were for what she had suffered. The meaning became implicit that she was no longer Samantha Crow but was Widow Samantha Goodson with independence and had the right to run her own affairs. There were many questions in the days to come and she found the strength to give thoughtful answers with a patience that she had not possessed earlier. Samantha hoped the new understanding would last.

Chapter 14

The Gravestone
On the river road, Late September 1783

Isaac had inquired about rock quarries and found that the only gravestone business was inside a farrier shop where a stone business was set up by the brother of the farrier. Isaac was set to take Samantha and Matthew there, which was a reasonable distance away.

"Isaac, maybe we could ask Auntie Geneva to watch Little Margaret so that Catherine could ride out with us. She may like the idea and would only have baby Henry with her since he has to be nursed. She will undoubtedly enjoy looking in the milliner shop with me. What do you think?" Samantha said.

"I would certainly enjoy having her go. Let me ask her," he said.

It was all setup for a trip to the stone chiseler to take place in two days. Samantha was sure Matthew was excited about going and she was glad his mind was busy with the importance of it. Father quietly told Samantha that he believed Matthew had perked up. It helped her feel better to bring him along on it, but it was not easy when grief hit her anew. Her pain of loss was newer than it was for the entire family who, months earlier, had attended laying Jonathan in the ground.

They left after breakfast on the appointed day and even Samantha was in a festive mood since Catherine was on an outing with them. Auntie and Grandmother had insisted on packing bread, apples, and cider for their dinner. They were happy to set out in the buckboard. It took the better part of an hour to find the location of the farrier along the Ohio River Road going back in an easterly direction past the point where they had arrived 10 days ago from lower Virginia. The village they entered was hardly isolated since the whole river bank along the Ohio River Road was teaming with settlers' camps. The population was waiting for safe entry into Ohio Country after conclusion of the Treaty of Paris signing they longed for. They were all living as close to the river as they could get and waiting.

The buckboard was pulled up to the hitching post and Isaac attached the lead rope to it. They walked into the barn where the collection of different shapes and sizes of granite stones were displayed. Isaac and Catherine were obviously enjoying the rare outing together. Samantha blushed happily when she could not miss the signs of their fleeting amorous glances for each other. The couple hung back so that Samantha and Matthew could conduct their business.

"I'm going to look at a smaller type of buggy. We'll be in the other side of the barn with the farrier. If you need us, we are not far," Isaac said as they turned to walk away. A nod from Samantha signaled her agreement.

"Look for the stone you like the best, Matthew," Samantha said.

Matthew walked slowly along with Samantha until he came to a darker gray one with light colored marbling running through it. He stood on one foot and put the tip of the other boot on the stone rectangle. "I like this one," Matthew said.

"It's the best choice here. It is attractive but masculine," Samantha said. "Now we have to see if our inscription will conform to the flat area showing."

A scruffy bearded man had watched them walk along the row of stones. "That the one you set your sights on, Miss?" he said.

"We are not sure yet, but we are ready to talk it over," Samantha said.

"You got money to pay for it, Miss?" the man asked.

"It may be customary to introduce yourself before you become so judgmental," Samantha said.

The man bowed low at the mere prospect of a paying customer and whipped his hat off. His red rim of gray streaked hair framed a bald head. "I am the proprietor of this fine stone shop, by name of James Wiggins, Ma'am."

"I am Widow Goodson and this is my brother, Mr. Matthew Crow," she said. "We will discuss the price of this stone and the price of engraving, which will inform us of how many lines we may choose to have inscribed."

"This here is expensive, Ma'am, comes from England," James Wiggins said. He quoted the price of 7£ (pounds), 8 shillings.

"Well then, we are not interested. Our Virginia militia fought in this war and we did not fight so we can continue to send our money to England for goods," Samantha said.

192

"I misspoke, Ma'am. I remember it to be from a Virginia stone quarry," Mr. Wiggins said.

"Is the price suddenly reasonable then?" Samantha asked.

"Yes, Ma'am, half off to you, Ma'am," Wiggins said.

"I will agree to 3£ (pounds), 8 shillings, in order to do business," Samantha said. She looked wide-eyed straight at him and waited.

"You drive a hard bargain, Widow Goodson. A body's got to eat," he said.

"Then you will barter for meat and potatoes, Mr. Wiggins?" Samantha said.

"No, Ma'am, 3£, 8 shillings it is."

"And the epitaph engraving, what will it cost?" Samantha said.

"To you, Ma'am, it is our cheapest rate." he said.

"What price is that?" Samantha asked.

"Well now, first we must have the information for the inscription, Ma'am."

Samantha glanced at Matthew while Mr. Wiggins was speaking. She looked away to maintain her composure. The effort to refrain from laughter was evidently as hard for Matthew as it had become for Samantha. "Mr.

Wiggins, if you don't mind, my name is Samantha and you may use it," she said.

"Yes, Ma'am," he said.

Samantha had not improved the situation and she stiffened her resolve and her posture. "This is what the inscription should say." She pulled a notation paper from her pocket beneath a velvet plume. She laid it on the worn bench that James Wiggins leaned on.

Before he could take a look at Samantha's information, he spat tobacco into a cuspidor, which was sitting on the floor by the bench leg. He had perfect aim and brown teeth from his years of practice. "Now then, let me have a look," he said. His grin exposed missing teeth.

Matthew was interested in the words Samantha had on the paper. She had written some of Mother's words explicitly to convey sentiments felt for Jonathan. There had been no trouble agreeing on them.

Jonathan Crow 1765 – 1783
Beloved Son, Grandson, Brother
Died Universally Lamented in
Year 18 of His Life.
Fought at Yorktown, Virginia Militia

"Ma'am, he died at Yorktown, you say?"

"No, Mr. Wiggins, Sir. The battle of Yorktown was 1781. He lived for two more years. This merely notes his patriotism on his tombstone," Samantha said.

"He a relative of yours, Ma'am?"

"He is my brother, Mr. Wiggins, Sir." Samantha stopped herself from the impulse of toe tapping. One look at Matthew and she knew she could not look at him again. He stood with his head tipped back and his gaze on the rafters with hands in his pants pockets. She half expected him to start whistling and she would surely lose it.

"May I have a price, Mr. Wiggins, Sir?" she asked.

Matthew cleared his throat and broke in with an idea, which he was urgent to present. "Samantha, there is room for one more thing," he said. "You could put that special heart symbol of Jonathan's on there, the one he made for you." He pointed with his finger to the spot he had in mind. "It would fit right after the word life."

"I love that idea, Matthew. Thank you." She drew the double-heart symbol carefully within the line of words and smiled at Matthew who wore a full grin.

"Well, now, that changes the price, Ma'am, but some of it may not fit on the stone," Mr. Wiggins said.

"Please give me a price, Mr. Wiggins," Samantha said.

He named a price of 3£ for every 40 letters. He had an intense focus with his squinty eyes. He chewed his tobacco fast with his bearded chin jutting out as he waited.

Samantha counted letters totaling 115, which would have to be cut back. She crossed out what she thought they could do without. Three lines instead of five resulted as she pared it down. She designated the double-hearts to be small and placed right after Lamented.

Jonathan Crow 1765 – 1783
Beloved and Lamented ♡♡
Yorktown, Virginia Militia

"I will pay 3£ total for 63 letters and the double-hearts," Samantha said and waited.

"Agreed. The total is 6£ and 8 shillings to be paid at once," he said.

"I will pay one pound now and the balance when it is satisfactorily completed," she said.

"Agreed," Mr. Wiggins said.

"How soon will it be ready to pick up?" Samantha asked.

"Near as I can tell, about one week," Mr. Wiggins said.

Samantha put one pound on the bench. "I will need a receipt, please." She reminded him of her name.

She placed the receipt in her pocket and thanked James Wiggins, promising to be back in the time agreed upon, exactly one week. It would be hard to wait.

Chapter 15

Good Deals
The Buggy, October 1783

Isaac and Catherine were anxious to show Samantha a buggy, which only two people could ride in and it required only one horse. "It would be a sensible model for travel to certain places, easier than a bigger wagon or buckboard. This will not fit my family, but for you, Samantha, it would do quite well if you think about it. You could ride out to help someone in need of a midwife, or to administer care for injuries. You could start a practice," Isaac said.

Samantha laughed out of pleasure for the confidence the statement thrust upon her by her friend. "I may do that but I am not ready yet. First, I must get beyond the distress of Jonathan's death. Let me look the conveyance over," she said as she walked closer. She felt the stare of the man who owned the farrier shop and looked up to see a man who looked exactly like James Wiggins, except he was wearing different clothes. She noted mentally that they must be twins.

She began purposely shaking her head no as she walked around the vehicle. It wouldn't do to let the proprietor know that she had fallen in love with the buggy in spite of its dusty condition. But she was thinking of how her horse, Brown, could effortlessly pull the small conveyance. She noted that there was an enclosed box for feet to rest and keep her black bag safe from falling. She would inquire at least on the price. She walked closer to the bench that the farrier was leaning on and was greeted with his noxious odor, which was beyond rank. He was as unkempt as his brother, James. She steeled herself not to careen away from the insult to her senses and asked, "Is this buggy spoken for or still for sale?"

"A mere 50£ will steal it from me," he said.

Her mind silently recorded, *No, you are trying to steal from me.* "Such generosity can only be met with a true offer of 1£," Samantha said.

He recoiled as if insulted and spat expertly into his cuspidor. Samantha also wanted to recoil. "Perhaps I will look elsewhere since I am sure to find another trap in better repair," she said. She did not know what the price should be and needed to find out by her own wits.

"The price stands firm at 12£, 5 shillings," he offered anew.

"I will agree on 5£, 5 shillings if it is cleaned to a shine, the weak stepping bar replaced, and it is ready to be picked up in one week," Samantha said. "Otherwise it cannot be driven away."

He shook his head no, just as she had, and pronounced it, "Sold."

Samantha decided the two brothers were just alike and predictable. She expected he would be asking for the full price up front like his brother. She preempted his request and put forth 5 shillings. "The balance will be paid upon satisfactory conditions met at the time of taking ownership. Please sign a receipt for my down payment. Widow Goodson is the name," she said. "You may want to write it on a tag as you reserve the chaise for me."

"John Wiggins at your service, Ma'am," he said as he wrote the receipt and signed his name.

The four walked back into the street. Catherine said, "I see the milliner shop a few doors down and I am keen to go in since I am not as sure of being with you next trip, Samantha." They were both glad to walk down the dusty roadway to glimpse inside the shop. They glanced back at Isaac and Matthew, who remained by their wagon but did not summon them to a shop they would have no interest in. The two friends stepped inside the store, and Samantha saw something she would have use for, but wondered if she would have to ask Grandmother how much to buy for the purpose she had in mind. She thought about it and asked for 10 yards of the white lace to be cut. She felt sure it would be enough for both purposes she had in mind. She was smiling as Catherine tried on a coquettish little hat.

"You look beautiful in the hat, Catherine," she said. "It will go well with one of your new dresses."

They looked at each other in amazement that they had not yet thought of a reason to wear the clothes. "Perhaps we will feel more special to wear them by Christmas season," Catherine said.

"We will have to coax Auntie into wearing one, since it is a momentous step for her," Samantha said.

"You are right about Auntie," Catherine said. "I will not get this hat since my old one is still not noticeably worn and serves me fine. There is a purchase you may want to make, Samantha."

"Oh...what do you mean?" Samantha asked.

"You and Auntie would undoubtedly feel warmer if you had cotton stockings and garter belts to hold them up," Catherine said.

They both smiled and Catherine helped Samantha select the right sizes for both of them. "This cold country requires them," Catherine said.

Samantha's white lace was rolled so no creases would result and it was wrapped in paper and tied with string. She envisioned putting it in the trunk Jonathan had made for her so long ago with double-hearts carved beside her name. She was happy to place it in the wagon for the trip home. She rode in the second seat of the wagon with Matthew and felt guilty that she had forgotten her sorrow for a short while and had enjoyed herself.

They had another enjoyment as they stopped at an overlook resting point jutting out into the river, providing a beautiful view of the water and the ferry boat. Picnic dinner seemed to taste so much better on their trip than around the table at home. Samantha was sure it was a pleasant experience for Matthew.

The shoppers were back long before supper and anxious to tell of success with ordering the stone for Jonathan's grave. The full reports from the day would wait until later when supper was done and children's prayers were heard.

All of the adults would hear the news together from Samantha and Matthew. Samantha wanted Matthew to be involved in the telling of it for everyone to hear

William Crow announced the agenda for the gathering and said they were all waiting to hear from Samantha and Matthew about the details of the gravestone. He added his thanks to Samantha's that the Hogans had taken them on their quest for the granite.

"Matthew picked the handsomest stone available, and I was pleased the minute he spotted it," Samantha said.

He couldn't hide his enjoyment of his sister's words. He joined in by reporting his amazement at Samantha having the money to purchase what she needed to buy. In his excited animation, he said, "Samantha bought a buggy for Brown to pull and we go get it in one week on the same trip to get the tombstone."

Samantha was pleased that he was planning on going with her again and was glad to have made her little brother happy by including him in worthwhile activity to keep his mind on.

"Mother, the price of stone inscription was rather high. We found it necessary to take some words off to make room for the most important information. The second line is your beautifully formed phrase, *Beloved and Lamented,*" Samantha said.

"Were you able to leave his militia service on the stone?" Father asked.

"Yes, Father," she said. "Of course, the first line is his name and dates." Everyone nodded approval.

Every member of Samantha's family thanked her for her generosity to purchase the stone. She said she was glad to do it. "Matthew proved his eye for detail with the greatest idea ever. He showed me where the double-heart symbol would tuck right in at the end of the middle line of the epitaph," she said. Matthew couldn't hide his pride in his sister's praise, his face beaming in a broad grin.

"Samantha made good deals," Matthew said, adding his excited opinion.

Her smile was as wide as Matthews. She was happier still that he had shared his opinion with everyone.

"I agree that she made smart deals," Isaac said while Catherine smiled her agreement.

Uncle Percy hadn't forgotten at all, something that he was responsible for bringing with them from their former life in southern Virginia. "Miss S'manthy, have you thought about those rose cuttings we decided to bring with us after propagating?" he said. "I've watered them faithfully and their roots should expand well wherever we put them in the ground to grow. I can't hold them over much longer without putting them into proper soil."

"Oh dear...I had not thought of it once," she admitted.

"They should have a chance to establish before the winter cold sets in, the only way to save them," he said.

"It was your excellent idea to bring them, Uncle Percy, and we don't want to lose them now," she said. "You put in the work to make sure we could have them."

"I might have saved some thyme plants, too, if they survived the trip," Percy said.

"Gram, you must be happy to know about the cuttings brought with us," Samantha said. "All of my friends know that they were your beautiful roses at the Crow farmstead."

"We lived there on the farm for several months, Grandmother Crow, and they were lovely," Catherine said.

Grandmother's smile complimented her words. "This is a sweet note in the midst of the sadness we have had," she said.

"We may want to plant one beside Jonathan's grave up the hill," Percy said.

"Yes. How wonderful," Grandmother said. She was content as she rocked and smiled.

"They can be dug up or propagated again to carry to Ohio Country, but this will save them for when the time comes," Percy said.

"I am so pleased you will take care of this, Uncle Percy," Samantha said, "unless you need me."

"He won't need you, Samantha, unless you plan on pushing me away from helping with the job," Isaac said, quite amused with his statement.

William was not to be left out. "I'll be right there to help decide where to put them, all but the one or two for Jonathan's grave. Mother Crow, will you look them over and decide on the healthiest ones for the graveside, maybe one for each side?" he said.

"Yes," she said, nodding her head for approval. She was happy that the roses she was responsible for years ago, had been brought and now they would serve a heartfelt purpose.

Marilla nudged her husband's arm. He looked at her and said, "Marilla had something to ask, which she could not forget." He had made an opening for her to speak.

"I had a rumor passed along to me today from my cousin," Marilla said, looking at Samantha. "He said that a young woman of your description, coming into the area in a caravan, shot a diamondback snake and killed it. Then it was said that you had a medical bag and doctored the young boy bitten by the poisonous snake. Was that really you, Samantha?" she asked.

"Yes, Mother. I did it on impulse and the boy probably had no chance otherwise," Samantha said. "I have regularly studied in medical books and the procedure for snake bite was there to learn. I am compelled to continue learning, healing, and doctoring, perhaps to begin again soon, especially if the need arises as this one did."

Samantha had made a decision that she would bring her black bag of doctoring tools with her wherever she went. If she could help someone, she would. That couldn't happen if she went about unprepared. She was not advertising it, but she would be ready.

"I am glad you were able to help the boy," Mother said. "But the shooting of the snake, they say it was a handgun used. Is that true, Samantha?"

Samantha was not sure if Mother was accepting of it or not, but the truth was the only thing she had to offer. "Yes, Mother. I have a handy little flintlock, which I will be glad to show you sometime."

"Since all of the younger children are sleeping, sometime can be right now," Mother said.

Samantha couldn't help but wonder if the inquiry from Mother was only curiosity in need of satisfaction or a question with consequence. She would find out. She stood up and reached into her pocket beneath the navy plume and produced her gun to satisfy Mother. She heard Mother's quiet gasp as the gun came into view. "This is loaded with black powder but will not shoot before it is cocked," Samantha said. "Of course I will not demonstrate that."

Grandmother had stopped rocking as if she also was wondering what Marilla's opinion was. She couldn't wonder more than Samantha, who was a bit worried, but trying not to let it show. Matthew was making no attempt to hide his interest. Samantha knew he was enthralled with the whole idea of the flintlock and she was also certain she should hide her own pleasure with his open approval. If it were going badly for her, it would only add fire against her missteps.

Mother smiled, which was a relief but would stiff words follow to wipe away Samantha's hope?

"I would like to shoot it, Samantha, when the time comes to allow it," Mother said. The rocking chair was moving and Samantha could almost breathe again. She hadn't realized she had suspended her breath until she worked hard to let it out inconspicuously. She did manage it.

"You are good with a musket, Mother, and you will find that this is accurate for close range. I have used it successfully enough two times and I was never as certain of my mark yet as you are with a musket," she said. "I will enjoy watching you shoot it," Samantha said.

"Samantha, I owe you an apology and I won't feel right until I say it," Mother said.

The rocking chair stopped along with all other thoughts that anyone else had, especially Samantha's suspension of belief. Matthew looked to be in disbelief but not more than Samantha. His mouth went lax again.

"I said something that I am sorry for and should not have said when you arrived here to find out that your brother had left this earth. It hurt you when I said you could not know the pain of a mother's loss of her firstborn because you had never been married. I should not have said anything of the kind and I understand now. Your grandmother and I have read a little more of your diary each day and compared them with the newspaper reports you clipped. We know what you faced and I am sorry for the hurtful remark. I don't mean to seem harsh and I know you hurt over Jonathan. I am very proud of you and congratulate you on your bravery and independence," Mother said. She looked directly at Samantha and spoke with sincerity.

Samantha stood up and hugged Mother. "Thank you. I love you, Mother. I knew you meant well but didn't have the information that you do now."

Everyone seemed happy and glad to talk about details of whatever came to mind. One of the details was the cooler nights and the need to have enclosed shelter for the winter. Samantha remembered the line in Jonathan's letter, which said a winter coat would be required. Now she saw the truth in that.

There was more that they needed.

"Before we are done with this meeting, I suggest it is in the best interest of all of us to stay together here for as long as our situation of waiting dictates. There are no available places for new arrivals. We all get on well as a group and can expand this building enough to make the space work," William Crow said. "Marilla and I agree that we will be happy to continue to make all of you welcome here. A discussion is necessary soon if everyone is to come to an agreement. We will consider the details together to carry out such a plan." He closed the meeting.

It was time to turn in and the three wagon beds stood ready as usual for Samantha and her friends.

Chapter 16

Colder Weather
October 1783

October began its beautiful autumn days with leaves in vibrant yellow and red hues. The days were somewhat warm, but the chilly nights pushed the urgency of the work for cutting trees of particular sizes to add space for bedrooms to enlarge the small cabin. It was bursting at its seams with the Crow family and friends. The decision was made by everyone that building on was the best way to make it through the winter for all of them.

The next evening the whole group was ready to discuss plans for the winter. "We are all moving on when the Virginia Military District land is marked out in our coveted Ohio Country," William Crow said. "That temporary nature will make our accommodations here less significant. We can build onto the cabin, small enough space to make-do while keeping life and limb warm and safe for the winter," he said. It was decided that William, Percy, and Leroy would get started on the work, without full help, for the one day that others had already planned a necessary trip.

Samantha, Matthew, and Isaac made the trip to bring the gravestone and the buggy home. While they were near the milliner shop, Isaac enlisted Samantha's help to purchase a particular hat for Catherine and they swore Matthew to secrecy, as it was to be kept for a Christmas present. Samantha found decorative hand mirrors, brushes, and hair combs to hold long hair fast. She purchased the available sets for Mother, Catherine, and Auntie Geneva. Her eyes sparkled as she stepped lightly up to the counter to pay for her purchases.

Matthew's eyes popped. "Mother never had such a set," he said.

"You are not to tell even Father," Samantha said.

"I won't tell. Wait, Samantha. Did you forget Grandmother," he asked.

"No, not at all, Matthew. Remember that I made a purchase on our first trip? It was white lace that I bought. It will be used for

Grandmother's sachets and something else for me," she said.

"What else for you?" Matthew said.

"I have a dress made of white velvet over bone color satin. It needs white lace trim over the satin. Grandmother may agree to do it for me when the time comes for a wedding dress," Samantha said.

"Whoa!" was Matthew's reply.

Isaac had finished with his shopping when Samantha asked him and Matthew to wait for her outside while she finished up in the milliner shop. They had no desire to stay longer. Isaac said he had business further down the street that he wished to do before he and Matthew would return, so they could all go to the farrier shop for the gravestone and the chaise.

Samantha was sure that neither Isaac nor Matthew had seen the snake skin she took into the milliner shop with her, rolled loosely in a piece of cloth and tucked under her arm. She left it to have a belt made for Isaac, wallets for Father and Uncle Percy, and knife sheaves for Leroy and Matthew. She was aware that Isaac owned one of the new style wallets, and just as sure that Father and Uncle Percy did not. After discussing it with the milliner shop proprietor, and getting good advice, she left instructions for complimentary leather to be used instead of the snake skin on undersides and insides of items. It left ample amounts of snake skin showing on the surface of all of the gifts.

The tail end rattler would be returned to Samantha with some of its own snake skin still attached. She ordered plain leather to be added to the underside of the skin for a medallion affect where it would adhere to any surface. She wanted it fastened in some form to her medical bag or to the chaise and was not yet sure which one. It was a large order for the shop and she paid some money up front while promising the balance when returning for the items in the third week of December. She was very pleased with the plans she had for Christmas gifts with the intention to make mittens for the younger children.

A meeting was held that same evening after their return from shopping. Isaac said he had important news for the entire household. It was taken as good news when he said he had gained a lawyer's privilege and gathered news on the day's trip. Isaac had gotten more information on the land tracts to be claimed. "William, you will be able to claim 100 acres as a former militiaman," he said. Isaac kept a list showing the information. "If Samantha's Corporal Sutter is going to claim land, which seems likely, it will also be 100 acres. The area claimed can then be settled, but some or all of a claim could be sold for the money. That is where others like me would be able to buy land for themselves, from settlers who would claim it only to sell. It is their perfect right to do so," he said. "Catherine and I hope for a place near the Crow family." Heads nodded as Percy and Geneva hoped the same, but Percy and Leroy would need to hire out for hard labor before they would have money to buy even a small property stake.

"Naturally, I hope to be near them, too, if Daniel Sutter is of the same mind, but a wife must go where her husband goes," Samantha said. *Was the slight move of Mother's head a warning of her disdain for Samantha's belief that Corporal Sutter would arrive?* Samantha's cheeks were heated as she trusted her instinct.

Isaac had another piece of information that he would not charge for. They all smiled as he said, "This is another contribution for the exceptional hospitality my family and I enjoy with the Crow family. This will save you money, Samantha," he said. "This is the gods' honest truth. There will be an ordinance in the Northwest Territory Treaty, which prohibits slavery. Language is being written into it that there will be no slavery or involuntary servitude allowed. It will mean that men of any color will be hired, not enslaved," he said. "It also means you do not have to draw up papers of freedom for Percy, Geneva, and Leroy. They are free when we cross the river and arrive in Ohio Country. It is a matter of useless payment for documents, which are not necessary."

Samantha turned to Auntie Geneva and her family and asked, "Are you able to accept this, Auntie, or would you feel better if I go ahead and have the papers drawn up for you?"

Auntie Geneva looked at Percy and then at Leroy. She seemed to read their minds since they did not speak, other than to shake their heads no.

"We trust the word we have just heard from Mr. Isaac and have never had reason to mistrust his word, Miss S'manthy. No money should be paid out for papers we will not need," Auntie said.

"Thank you, Isaac, Auntie, Uncle Percy, and Leroy," Samantha said. She made a mental note for herself that maybe she would tuck the saved money into Uncle Percy's new wallet to help them. She had to be careful how she gave something because they had their pride and were not too proud to work.

"I do want to request that several of us go up the hill to place the gravestone on Jonathan's grave before we start work tomorrow," Samantha said.

Father agreed that it would be first on the agenda after breakfast in the morning. Grandmother rocked and William said, "We will be taking the marker up the hill in the wagon, Mother Crow, and you will ride with it. We will have a prayer over Jonathan's grave before we start the day of work."

All heads nodded in agreement.

"This meeting is over," Isaac said to all of the faces smiling at him.

The next day, the company of family and friends were ready to work to expand their lodging and accomplish warmth for the winter with additional enclosed space. William, Percy, and Leroy had premeasured the three bed frames inside the wagons the day before to be sure they were all exactly the same size. Only a three-foot width beside a bed would be added to the size inside of each room to be able to move inside the room with the bed placed inside. Their belongings could be kept under their beds as consolidated goods, much like they were in the wagons. They needed to store canned goods inside before the freezing weather sure to come.

The project began by girdling the trees, a process of scoring the trunks all the way around and removing the bark while the trees stood. A few had been done the previous day by William, Percy, and Leroy. The trees would die if they waited long enough, but they were in a hurry. Matthew worked day after day on the removed bark, pulling it a distance away from the trees on a wooden bobsled. Father gave him instructions and left him to his work. Matthew piled it in numerous standing teepee shapes. Air could circulate through it so it would dry for burning in the fireplace later. Several days passed as he worked to stand the bark upright.

The first teepee he had stacked was dry, and he started chopping it into smaller sections that he cut shorter for burning in the fireplace. Mother was very appreciative of the bark to start the cooking stove fire each morning and praised Matthew for good work. As more trees were debarked, his work continued and was as important as the men's work.

Logging had begun with William and Percy designated as having the strength and expertise to do the hard work of felling the naked trees. They used ropes and a pulley to guide the mules to load the raw wood cylinders on a wagon. When they arrived with a load at the cabin, they used the Jacks to drag logs into position.

Isaac and Leroy seemed to be good at measuring, marking, and using an ax to notch the log ends for slot connections to build the walls. They used pine pitch on the outside for cracks between logs because it would harden and not be washed away.

Catherine and Samantha mixed dirt and water into thick clay mud to fill inside between the beams. Some of Catherine's attention went to baby Henry for nursing.

The floors remained sod.

If land grants were not yet available by spring, the men planned to use mules to pull the roots left in the ground from the felled trees and clear off the land for more garden space. William discussed with everyone that all of their work on the trees were Indian methods he had learned of.

The project required the faithful preparation of food for hungry workers, food which Marilla, Geneva, and Priscilla kept under plentiful provision three times a day. Samantha and Catherine were able to help with dinner in the middle of each day and they needed a break from their harder labor.

Auntie took Samantha aside. "Miss S'manthy, I gave Gowdy's knife to Leroy, since he can make use of it with some trimming of logs where he and Isaac notch them. I wanted you to know he is making use of his uncle's knife and is honored to have it. He skinned a rabbit with it, too," she said. Samantha hugged Auntie.

Work went on day after day. The rooms with their roof in place were finished by October's end.

Samantha often thought of how nice it would have been to have Jonathan's help, and she missed him. She day-dreamed of the beautiful life she would have if Corporal Daniel Sutter were present. She had come back to the point of knowing that Jonathan would still want her to have that happiness. He had been the one to make possible, the note, accepting it from Daniel and giving it to her. She kept it in her pocket again. She happily pulled it out and read it each day, a bright spot again, reminding her of the future.

Chapter 17

Winter Challenge
Snow, November 1783

It was colder and snow flurries were common. November reminded Samantha of her need for a cloak. She wore two shawls around her shoulders when she went out riding in the trap. Brown had learned rather quickly to pull it with Samantha in the seat behind, directing him with the reins. She often had Matthew with her, but Father had cautioned them not to go far. Matthew would often shoot small game and skin it on the spot, taking only the meat and pelts home. They felt safe enough and extended their range more each time.

Mother was fond of having a little freedom, too, and often rode out with Samantha. They traveled on a planned visit to Mother's cousin's cabin, Lyle, and visited with his wife, Eloise. The visit was purposeful to have Eloise, a seamstress, measure Samantha for a hooded cape. The burgundy velvet garment's thick inside quilting for warmth was to have a thin silk innermost lining next to the body. "This will be ready in one week," Eloise said. Samantha was pleased to contemplate the warmth that the cloak would provide while being attractive in its design.

Eloise was pleasant enough but seemed to think Samantha had no mind of her own. "William should soon be able to find a husband for you," she advised Samantha.

"I am an independent widow and I expect Corporal Daniel Sutter to arrive here as my suitor when the Continental Army musters out," Samantha said.

Eloise seemed flustered and abruptly stopped the conversation. Samantha felt as uncomfortable as Eloise and Mother, wondering what Mother may have said to Eloise at some other time. Neither of them could have known of Samantha's status the last time they talked. Samantha understood that.

"This is information my family has just learned on my arrival here," she said. Samantha's words didn't seem to help and it was obvious that Eloise could not let go of her discomfort. "I will return for the cloak after the proper time has elapsed to allow for your work," Samantha said.

She began to wish they had not come and thought Mother would hold it against her for speaking up about her independence. She knew she was right when an uncomfortable silence prevailed on the ride home.

There was a time when she and Mother had an opportunity to shoot the flintlock. Mother seemed almost reluctant when her chance arrived. She developed the same throat clearing that Father sometimes had. Samantha could see that Mother felt guilty for asserting independence to do something so daring even though she did shoot it at a rabbit and missed. She preferred the musket, which they had with them at all times.

Whether accompanied by Mother or Matthew, it made no difference about caution. Samantha had the flintlock and her medical bag was always tucked under her seat.

Past the middle of November, after she had her warm cloak, a couple of inches of snow had fallen during one night. Matthew was riding with Samantha on the road that went out past the gravestone tree. There had been no wheel tracks, save the ones they were making.

They came across a slew of animal tracks, which cut across the road in a zigzag pattern. They were coyote tracks following the jackrabbit prints in the snow. Matthew pointed out that there had been lone horse tracks leading toward them, but they vanished when the coyote and rabbit tracks crossed them. It was then that they heard a cry for help. They stood still and listened until a weaker call came again.

"It's off the side down that culvert, Sam. Let me look," Matthew said. In his excitement, he jumped down from the chaise. As he peered over the edge, Samantha smiled at his slip with her name. He had called her Sam and she approved of the reminder of what Jonathan had so often called her.

"There's a man down there and it is steep. I don't know how we can get to him," Matthew said. Samantha had gotten down from the trap and walked to the edge.

"It's good that Father said I should always carry a strong cord along with this two-wheeled wonder. We can throw the end down and he can tie it around himself so we can use the horse to pull him up. I'm sure Brown won't mind helping," Samantha said. "Matthew, use your loudest voice to holler down and ask if he can manage if we throw a rope down for him to tie on himself," she said.

"Hello mister. If we throw a rope down can you fasten it around you?" Matthew called with his hands cupped to project his voice down the precipice. There was no answer, so he tried again to get a reply. None came.

"Without a rope around him we can't bring him up," Samantha said.

"Lower me down, Sam. I can do it," Matthew said.

"No. You are not going down there, Matthew. Absolutely not," she said.

"But, Sam, you can let me down on the rope and I can tie it around him. When you get him up, you can throw a line to me to come back up," Matthew said.

It sounded reasonable, but something did not feel right about allowing Matthew to be in a vulnerable position. "I can't allow it until we have help. We will go home for help and come back. Maybe then Father will let you do it when there is more backup than just me to help you and the wounded man," Samantha said.

"I can do it, Sam. Let me try," Matthew pleaded.

"No. First let's mark the spot with something. What can we use?" she said.

"How about the rope?" Matthew said.

"No. Someone would love to steal it. There are pieces of wood around here to collect into a pile," Samantha said. She was ready to collect wood.

"I can gather twigs before you can get your skirts out of your way, Sam," Matthew said. He was right. He hurried to bundle an armload of sticks, which he placed on the spot where they looked down and saw the man who was not moving. They called one more time to say help was coming, but there was no answer.

"We are leaving so we can hurry back with some help," Samantha called to him.

They drove fast to get back to the cabin and found Uncle Percy, Leroy, and Father able to return with them in the bigger wagon. They would have a place to put the man if he were still immobile.

"Do you think he is dead, Samantha?" Father asked.

"I could have gone down all ready, but Samantha wouldn't let me," Matthew said.

She looked at Matthew but ignored his statement to Father in favor of answering the question.

"He wasn't dead when we first saw him, so he may be severely wounded and unconscious. I really can't tell until we get him up from the deep gulley. Since he can't help with the line, we have to send someone down the ravine with a rope and board so he can be fastened to it. We need to pull him up with such care that we do not cause more injury," Samantha said.

"Good point, Samantha. I will get a board and we can take an older blanket and some more rope to wrap and bind him," Father said.

The five of them rode in the wagon that Percy and Leroy had hurried to harness up with horses to pull it. Matthew spotted the mound of sticks first and let them all know that they had arrived. The five of them stood at the rim of the gully in the footprints made by Samantha and Matthew earlier.

Father cupped his hands around his mouth, projecting his voice down the canyon. "Hello, down there. Hello," he called. There was no answer. "Well, looks like we will work hard to get him out to see if he can be helped in time," Father said. "And, by the way, Samantha, you made an excellent decision to keep Matthew out of that deep crack in the earth," he said.

Samantha was smiling, but Matthew was shaking his head.

"Leroy, you are the strongest candidate to try going down this steep incline," Percy said. "What do you think of going down?"

"I figured the same thing as long as it involves a rope tied to the wagon to give me an anchor to keep from falling like that poor fellow down there," Leroy said.

They were all smiling in agreement except for Matthew. Percy tied knots at three intervals on the end of the rope Leroy would use to hold onto as he made his descent.

"Matthew, turn the team around to face the rim but stay back a distance and we'll see how long the line allows for letting it down gradually. We can bring the horses forward a step or two at a time as Leroy goes down," Father said.

Matthew was glad to help and jumped at the chance to have his own job assigned by Father. Samantha was relieved that Father didn't leave him out after she had prevented him going down into the dark crevasse.

They all agreed that Leroy should not be tied to the rope since he was strong and muscular. "He could get tangled in the rope and become strangled," Percy said.

William and Percy kept control of the horse's slow steps forward to let Leroy down. They stood on each side of the horses with a firm grip on their bridles. They talked quietly and patiently to the animals as they stopped and started.

"Whoa, whoa boy," Father said.

Finally, the line slacked and gave notice that Leroy had reached the bottom. They peered over the edge to hear Leroy call up to them, saying they could pull the stringer up. "Fasten the musket on the board and send it down. There is an injured horse down here," Leroy called out. It was a slow process as they let the board and gun down by hand.

They heard Leroy's shot from below.

They waited while Leroy bundled and bound the injured person onto the board like a papoose. He gave a strong holler when he had the man ready to be pulled up. He was brought up at a slow pace with the help of one horse taken from the team. They walked the work animal slowly away from the edge to ease the bundle upward. The precarious instability of the situation was strictly watched by Samantha as she waited to see if she had a patient who could be helped, or if they merely had a body.

Uncle Percy and Matthew steadied the board as it came over the bank and could be laid flat on the ground. Percy signaled William to pull the bundle further away from the edge for a better spot to let Samantha take a look at the injured man. He untied the patient and made another knot in the rope for a holding point for Leroy. Father brought the horse closer and turned him around to go away from the edge of the precipice again. They were ready to help Leroy ascend the height of the fissure. Matthew was glad to be the one to throw the braided sisal over the side.

Samantha had felt for a pulse and found it to be weak before she pulled back the blanket to see what the injuries were. She could see at least one broken bone to be stabilized and more have to be suspected after such a fall. The worst wide open gashes needed immediate attention. She bound his head with sheeting to try to curtail bleeding from a deep wound. She needed to get him to a warm cabin and take proper care of him. Matthew watched her feel every inch of the man's arm and press down on it to push the bone back in line before using a piece of Matthew's wood gathered earlier. She wrapped sheeting firm to splint the arm into a stationary condition. "Thank you, Matthew," she said to acknowledge his contribution.

"It is best to push the bone in place while he is still knocked out," Samantha said.

Father, Leroy, and Percy were leaning over them now.

"The horse in the gully had a broken leg and most likely a broken neck. I had to put him away," Leroy said. The colorful horse blanket Leroy held was an Indian blanket taken from the horse along with a bridle.

The injured man hadn't moved, nor opened his eyes, or said a word. "Is he alive?" Matthew asked.

The three men gave a nervous chuckle at the blunt question.

"He is alive," Samantha said for Matthew's benefit. "I feel a faint pulse."

"We can load him in the wagon when you give the order," Father said to Samantha.

"Yes, please, but he has to be strapped to the board again. With that severe head wound, we have to keep him stationary as he may have injuries not realized yet. We need to get him where it is warm," she said. The injured man was carefully lashed to the board again and lifted into the transport wagon by the three men and a boy.

They started for home with the man pulled from the depths. He had a chance of survival and they wanted to find out who he was in case he had a family. His business suit was curious and a pocket watch was still dangling from a gold chain, which Samantha pushed back into his pocket. Curiosity was secondary to finding out if he had a family expecting him home. They assumed that he had ended up at the bottom of the ravine when the horse was spooked by the coyote running a rabbit.

At the cabin, the man was carried inside. They decided he could be put in Matthew's bed. Matthew was agreeable to sleeping on the floor near the fireplace. He was still doing his part to help the man every way possible.

"Miss S'manthy, that's a lot of blood soaking through the band you wrapped around his head," Auntie Geneva said.

"Yes it is. I need to take it off now and rinse the wound before I apply a thicker bandage and compress it with another wrap. It is an egregious injury full of dirt and gravel," she said.

"I'll help you, Miss S'manthy. We need a basin to catch the water as it pours over the wound. I'll be right back," Auntie said.

234

"I think I should rinse wine over it after the water and make sure grit and gravel wash out well," Samantha said.

They were a close knit team as they worked on the man to clean him up and bandage the biggest flesh gashes. The head injury was last and they braced themselves when it was uncovered and ready to have water washed over it to remove debris. Uncle Percy and Father held onto the man in case he would come to himself when the water was poured. He did not react to cold or pain when water poured into the open wound. It pushed Samantha's decision to go ahead and pour wine over it for better cleansing since the water they used had not been boiled. They held him fast as Samantha and Auntie bound his head again to cover the angry hole in his head. He remained as comatose as when they started. They had all seen the horrendous wounds to his skull and brain and held no great hope for his survival.

Samantha checked his pulse again. "It continues to beat. I can't say how long it will be present. I also think it will be a miracle if he is not moonstruck from the consequence of this deep wound," she said. Auntie nodded her agreement. "He requires watching around the clock, I believe," Samantha said.

"I will help and that miracle you mentioned, Miss S'manthy, I don't think we will see it," Auntie Geneva said.

"We can do our best," Samantha said.

"You would never do less, Miss S'manthy," Auntie said.

Mother and Catherine had put supper on two platters in the center of the table and they all enjoyed cider, bread, and apples. They needed to talk about the wounded man after the children were in their beds. They would begin only when Grandmother was in her rocker and Catherine sitting down to join them.

Chapter 18

Identity Inquiry
December 1783

The injured man's clothing had been hung on the line to dry with the torn cloth, melted snow, and blood apparent. It was beyond salvage of any mending skills. "The clothing should be dry before being wrapped and saved to give to his family if one is found. Otherwise, the clothing will mold," Mother insisted.

The striped horse blanket lay in the middle of the table, which they all gathered around. William Crow picked up the gold watch and chain. "This expensive timepiece is a clue that this man has means and connections. The initials S.G. inscribed on the back should be our guide. It may provide a way to find his family if we inquire about him having this watch along with the colorful horse blanket," he said.

"We need to be cautious about showing around an expensive watch on a chain," Isaac said. "Some dishonest folks will want to claim it for the money it will bring."

"You know that's right," Percy said.

"We are all agreed on the folly of showing the watch around to find the owner then," William said. "But the blanket is different than plainer ones generally in use. We could safely use that to see if anyone recognizes who the owner is while listening for clues about the initials S.G.," William said. "Who is willing to go down the river road tomorrow to inquire all along the way to try to find out who this man is and where he belongs?"

They all looked around at each other.

"I will. I have some business anyway on that busy stretch. It may also help business to introduce myself to as many new folks as possible. Anybody volunteering to go along with me?" Isaac said, as they all smiled, acknowledging his gift of gab.

"I believe I could spare the time to keep you company," Leroy said.

Isaac reached across the table to shake Leroy's hand.

It was decided on how to search for the man's relatives. Now everyone would sleep soundly except for Samantha and Auntie Geneva. They took turns sitting beside the injured man's bed and were able to doze off and on when it was their turn to watch the patient. The man had a pulse, but no activity, which indicated that he was in a coma as far as Samantha could tell. She did not always doze off, but studied a medical book about coma's and the outcomes that could happen, not all of them good. She worried about the brain swelling that would more than likely occur.

When Isaac and Leroy were ready to leave in the morning, Samantha asked, "Please also inquire if there is an experienced doctor who could come and look at this man. If there is more that should be done for him, we will help him better to the benefit of saving him for his family."

"We will do as you ask, Samantha, but it seems doubtful if there is more to be done, other than to wait to see if he makes it. We won't give substantial hope on that if we find his family, since you said it was uncertain," Isaac said.

"I think it would be wrong to give much hope, but it will give his family a chance to see him before he expires, if they can be found right away," Samantha said.

~~*~~

It was after dinner in the middle of the day when Isaac returned with the horses and wagon. Leroy was not with him. Isaac looked around for William and Percy, who were working on wood to burn in the fireplace. He motioned for them to come inside where he could tell everyone at once about his news.

In no time, everyone gathered at the table, anxious to hear Isaac's news and find out why Leroy did not return.

"We found the man's family, a wife and five children. His name is Simon Gray and he was a captain for General George Washington's Continental army. Leroy stayed back in order to work on chopping wood for the woman's cabin. The wood was used up and Mrs. Gray's oldest, a boy of age 11, was using an ax to try to keep enough wood ahead of what they had to burn. Leroy, with his strapping muscular build, is helping out, as the boy is frail. It is a huge good deed he is doing for the family," Isaac said and took a breath.

"Is the family waiting to go to Ohio Country like most of the folks along the river road?" William asked.

"That is right and we didn't tell Mrs. Gray that he may never make it. We said he was in a weak state but being well cared for. She can't leave those children alone and I said I would be back with one of the women from our household to stay with them so she can ride back here. I also need Percy or William to go so she can be brought here with her husband's own rig, which I will explain. But first, who will go?" Isaac asked.

Marilla and Geneva both spoke up at the same time. Samantha's heart swelled with pride that her mother would volunteer. Geneva said she believed Marilla should bundle up and go help the woman with her children.

"I did inquire about the need for a doctor, Samantha. There is one at some distance west from us and they said he is seasoned but excellent when he can get to the patient," Isaac said. "You made it clear that it would be dangerous to the patience's health to be moved from here," Isaac said.

"Yes, he is critical and that doctor is needed as soon as possible," Samantha said. "Seasoned? What does that mean?" she asked.

"It could mean old or slow or both, maybe experienced, or something entirely different. Maybe I'll know if I find him. I will go to look for him after I return to Mrs. Gray with help from here. I will continue on down the river road and seek him out," Isaac said. "That is the reason for the need of another driver to bring her with her own rig back here."

"I will go," William said. It was settled. He and Marilla were ready to ride back with Isaac, heading down the road to assist Mrs. Gray, who was anxious to come to her husband's side.

It was nearly an hour before William returned with a woman who seemed timid. Later they knew the timidity was her fear of what she would find. It was worse than she had dared to guess. Samantha told her of the deep head wound and his continuing coma.

"The coma is possibly a blessing to keep him still and sedated," Samantha said. "We have word of a doctor west of here and Isaac has gone to locate him and try to bring him here tonight if it is possible. We assume that doing all that can be done for Mr. Gray is the desirable action to take."

"Yes, without fail. If only he can recover." Mrs. Gray got over her breathless shock and stepped closer. She had clutched at her chest as a first reflex but now her wide open hand came down. She reached toward his fist, hesitated and then took his hand in hers. He gave no response and appeared as if sleeping. Mrs. Gray started sobbing and took two steps back with her hand over her mouth.

Samantha spoke to the injured man to say his wife was with him. She remembered reading that sometimes people deep in a trance do hear what is said. He remained unresponsive as if nothing was heard or understood. Samantha pulled the chair nearer the bedside for Mrs. Gray and invited her to sit down. The woman sat suddenly as if her knees had been ready to collapse. Samantha stood by the door watching and letting the ill-fated woman acclimate to the situation of her husband. She had waited a good while before she spoke.

"I don't believe he will wake anytime soon, Mrs. Gray, just so you know. His body and head have been through a trauma. He has to heal and adjust slowly if he is to recover," Samantha said.

"Who applied these bandages and administered aid to take care of him?" Mrs. Gray asked.

"I have been doing it to the best of my ability, Mrs. Gray. We hope the inquiry to find a doctor with more training than myself is successful, but as a healer, I am doing my best for him," she said.

"Thank you, was it Samantha, I believe?" Mrs. Gray said. She went right on, "Do you think he will recover?"

"His chance is small, to be honest, Mrs. Gray. The wound in his head is horrendous," Samantha said.

Mrs. Gray was sobbing quietly, her mind busy with so much to consider. Her head was down on her chest. Samantha stepped to the bedside and patted her shoulder. Mrs. Gray had looked up and realized that Samantha was checking for a pulse in his neck. She misunderstood and let out one shriek as she ran away from her worst fear. She ran into the arms of Geneva in the doorway. Geneva sat her down on a chair by the table and held her as she sobbed.

Samantha knew the pulse was weak, but it was still there. She went with shaky legs to sit by Mrs. Gray. She comforted Mrs. Gray as they sat there. "He is hanging onto his shred of life and cannot be moved," she said. The situation of her husband had unnerved Mrs. Gray but

Samantha had a calm demeanor that could help.

Mrs. Gray raised her head. "I have five young children and possibly will not have a husband. We will not get to Ohio Country to claim our land. I do not know how we will manage," she said. She began to sob again but soon had to recover when new thoughts came. "I have to tell my children just how badly their father is injured. They knew when I left them with Marilla Crow, only that he had fallen off his horse. It will be hard for them to hear of him in such bad condition, but it must be done," Mrs. Gray said.

William, Matthew, and Percy had come inside when Catherine had opened the door to beckon them. There was a quiet discussion, while Catherine kept the Crow children and her two younger ones in her sleeping space to play with their dolls on the bed. Catherine stood in the doorway to listen to the group around the table.

William said, "There will be no harm in keeping Mr. Gray in the space he is in now and leave him undisturbed until he is better and can be taken home. Mrs. Gray, your children won't benefit from seeing him in such a bad state. Maybe a preacher's words would help you and the children. Does that sound like a good way to handle it, or are we meddling in something that we should let alone?" he said.

Mrs. Gray stood up and heaved a sigh, glad that a load had been lifted and relieved her from worry of having to move her husband. "Oh no, you are not meddling and I am grateful that you have extended help, which I could not have asked for or thought of. I must thankfully accept your help if you mean it. My thoughts have run far ahead in desperate concern for my children, but I must try to find a way to move forward. Today is quite enough," she said.

Percy spoke up. "Ma'am, my son is cutting wood for you. I understand it will get you over a rough spot. I can offer to help alongside him to get a bigger supply cut and bring you past this recuperation time for your husband. I hear that you have a woodshed that Leroy will stay in overnight so you are not alone on the property. We will send a bedroll to him and I will work with him tomorrow on wood to get further ahead on the supply for burning," he said.

Mrs. Gray was shaking her head in disbelief. "I need the help badly but hardly know how to accept it," she said.

"I have had some great help in my life from our friends here, Mrs. Gray. That is why my son and I want to give a hand. We have something to be grateful for and giving a hand to someone in need seems a good way to show it," Percy said.

Mrs. Gray could see every kind face in the room and felt the love surrounding her. She was shaking her head yes.

"If you have a night shirt for your husband that could be used you could send it back here tonight. He needs to be in unblemished clothing. The suit he had on is torn and bloody and will need to be replaced when he can go home," William Crow said. He had tried to cover everything.

"I can send a night shirt. I will arrange for the preacher we know, Minister Hartman, to come and talk with the children sometime tomorrow," Mrs. Gray said. She rose from her chair as if she was weary beyond her endurance. "I must get back to my children. They are waiting for word of their father and I have to tell them what troubled circumstance he is in."

William stood up to take Mrs. Gray back to her cabin. Geneva slipped a bedroll into

William's hands and said, "I put some wine, bread, apple, and venison in there for Leroy."

"I should at least feed him and I must feed my children, too. I will manage to do what has to be done," Mrs. Gray said.

"We will feed Leroy, Ma'am. You have your responsibility and we have more adults here to spread the work around," Geneva said.

Mrs. Gray had thanked everyone before she turned to go out the door with William.

"I don't envy her with an impaired husband and all those children. No, I don't envy her," Geneva repeated.

Chapter 19

Help Could Arrive
When? December 1783

William Crow returned Mrs. Gray safely home to her children. He and Marilla patiently listened while Mrs. Gray explained to her five children that their father was badly hurt and could not be moved. She remembered to send a flannel nightshirt back with them to be put on Simon. She understood that it would be cut down the center of the back so that it could be slipped on both arms and tucked under him. Nothing would be pulled over his head and disturb his wounds.

William and Marilla arrived home to the Crow cabin after supper was over. "Any sign of Isaac yet with that doctor we need?" William asked as he entered.

Percy shook his head grimly. "Miss S'manthy and Geneva are worried about the swelling of the man's head," he said. "It's not just the wound but the whole head."

Geneva stepped out from the sick room. "If it swells much more, Samantha believes he is in real trouble," she said. In the next breath she asked, "Did you speak with Leroy and see where he is sleeping? I hope that shed is fit enough that he can keep warm."

William laughed. "We did look inside the shed and it is actually an addition on the barn where a cow, horses, and some penned-up chickens are kept. An open door connects the two and Leroy has a soft bed in the straw. We are glad to report that it is comfortable and you don't need to worry," he said. "Leroy's presence there should be a relief for Mrs. Gray since he has fed the animals and carried water into the barn for them. There are plenty of jobs besides chopping wood and Leroy is not lazy. He is a son to be proud of."

Relief washed over Geneva as she smiled and nodded her head as pleased as Percy was.

"We are starting to wonder what the hold-up is for Isaac. His search for that doctor seems to be dragging out," Percy said.

"I believe we need patience with this waiting game. He had farther to go than the trip I made and had only word of mouth to go on. He will be asking questions of people west of here and if anyone can find that doctor, it is Isaac," William said.

Geneva sighed. "You are right but Simon Gray may be running out of time."

Samantha stepped out the door of the injured man's bedroom with a medical book she had been reading to find insight in helping her patient. "I am convinced that I do not have the experience needed to try a treatment for head and brain injury mentioned in these pages," she said. "We need a doctor to decide if the strategy mentioned here can be done and the ability to carry out the treatment if applicable. I have never seen bloodletting done and would never attempt it without firsthand knowledge of how to proceed," she said. "It is important to learn it when I have the opportunity and I hope our patient lives to have its benefit."

"I approve of your caution, Samantha," Father said. "We did bring the clean nightgown for the patient and it can be put on for added warmth. Isaac will help me put it on him so you and Geneva won't need too."

"Agreed," Samantha said as Auntie Geneva added her approval with a nod as she finished cutting it down the back.

Marilla busied herself with setting out bread, cider, and apples for a late meal for her and William. "I did not want to eat the food that Mrs. Gray has stored for her children even though I prepared supper for them," she said. "I worry that she may run out of food even with her supplies looking plentiful now. It is hard to say what the future will bring for her with so many children to feed," Marilla said.

Grandmother and Catherine habitually tucked children in bed earlier in the evening and it was naturally quiet as worry set in over the prolonged wait for Isaac to return. Catherine soon laid down with her restless children and Grandmother had to give up nodding off in her rocker in favor of her bed. Matthew was asleep beside the fireplace. Percy turned in with Geneva ahead of her time to sit up in a later hour with the patient. She wanted to be ready for her watch when Samantha needed to rest.

Samantha knew that Mother went to bed, but Father sat in a chair at the table, leaning forward in light sleep. She was comforted knowing he would rouse the moment Isaac returned. She was unwilling to doze off in the chair beside the patient's bed when he seemed so critical. She paced quietly to keep herself alert, continually checking the comatose man.

It was late, but Samantha still could not bring herself to wake Auntie Geneva to take over. She stopped pacing when she thought she heard some activity outside. She listened and was sure that she was correct in assuming it was Isaac, not just the wind rattling at the gate. There was light tapping on the door before the latch was lifted. Father stirred and was alert when Isaac entered. Samantha thought the man behind him was familiar. She struggled with her memory. She knew the man, who was grayer than she remembered. He used a stout cane with an eagle head carved on the crook of it. It added balance with a wooden leg that caused him to limp. He hadn't had either of them when she had seen him last. His name came to her with no doubt in her mind.

William Crow was smiling and had figured out the man's identity at the same time. He shook hands as soon as he could stride across the room. "Doc Murphy! Can it be you?" he said. "Welcome, welcome to the Crow home."

Doc gave a hearty laugh. "What a great visit we'll have," he said, "but only after I see the patient." William motioned toward the

253

doorway where Samantha stood. Doc Murphy made his way toward Samantha but seemed unable to recognize her. He stopped short and chuckled low in the way Samantha remembered from long ago at Yorktown camp. "Sam, is it you, Samantha?" He chortled in his throaty undertone again, with unmistakable pleasure. "I should have known you would grow up so well, Sam." Almost apologetically, Doc said, "You will always be Sam for me."

Samantha was speechless with her rosy cheeks and smile. She could not tell him she preferred her nickname, not now anyway.

Isaac took it in, seeing that there was a familiarity between the three. He had not mentioned the Crow name to Doc, who was taken by surprise on coming into their cabin. Isaac carried Doc's worn leather satchel and set it down beside the bed of the gravely ill patient. It was as old and beat up as its owner and could not be accidently mixed up with Samantha's black valise. Doc noticed her bag but was intent on assessing the patient, the reason he came.

"I was told the patient had exceptional treatment. Could that be you giving such critical care, Sam?" Doc asked while his crinkling eyes showed his pleasure.

"Yes, Doc, me and Auntie, but I know this man's life is at risk and I believe he needs more than the help of a healer and midwife. I am grateful you have come," Samantha said.

"Tell me what I need to know, Sam. I heard how this man was injured but tell me about his wounds and condition and what the most pressing need is," Doc said.

"It won't matter about his broken arm, deep cuts and bruises, and battered body if his horrendous head wound swells more inside his skull. I took care of those injuries, but I believe he will be moonstruck if he lives through this. You may need to see the site of his head trauma to decide if there is a helpful possibility. I have only read about bloodletting but have never done it and would not attempt it on my own," Samantha said.

"I do need to see it," Doc said as he took a seat and started carefully dismantling the bandage around the man's head. While he continued uncovering, he said, "Bloodletting is often necessary for brain injuries. How have you learned about it, Sam?"

"I study medical books almost daily," she said. Samantha motioned to Auntie Geneva to enter as she caught a glimpse of her just beyond the door, no doubt awakened by the voices and activity. "Doc, I have had help from Auntie Geneva and would like her to see everything that takes place here. She does half of the care and loses as much sleep as I do in order to never leave our patient unattended."

Auntie entered right away. "Auntie, I would like you to meet an old friend, Doc Murphy, whom I met at Yorktown battlefield," Samantha said. Auntie curtsied slightly as Doc acknowledged her with the incline of his head. He had reached the last layer of bandage removal and went to great pains to be careful of disturbing the wound as he finished.

"This wound is horrendous. Bloodletting will relieve pressure and has proved to be the most helpful in a case like this. The procedure will not change the outcome of the probable madness, according to the extent of his injury. It could be cruel and useless to try to help him live in such a state. However: we should do our best to help him and leave the rest to God," Doc said, looking straight at Samantha.

"He has a family that loves him, his wife and five children who have every hope that he will make it," Samantha said.

"We can try to keep him alive, but no guarantee in his perilous condition," Doc said. "You understand, Sam?"

"Perfectly well understood," Samantha said. Both Father and Auntie's heads were nodding. Father stepped out and brought two chairs before he took a seat again at the table where he would keep a distant watch. Isaac sat at the table drinking cider and eating bread.

"We can't be in a hurry and will need to heat water if a small amount if it can be arranged," Doc said. "Such a thing as boiled water was not possible in a battlefield camp but is possible here with a little patience."

Auntie elected to set a water pot on the stove, half-full, and Father stoked the coals with an iron poker before he added wood.

"While we wait for the water to heat, I'll lay out the instruments," Doc said. He opened his bag and began. "Sam, that's a handsome black valise you have. I assume it's yours?"

"Yes Doc. I plan on using the tools in it whenever needed although I have not been here long. This is the first instance of need that fell to me in this area."

"I believe there is need that I am unable to fill, lacking as my health is," Doc said. "Midwifery is not my domain. We could be of use to assist one other. You could build a practice and your reputation. I'd appreciate the help as I try to slow down and take better care of myself. I can't keep up the pace indefinitely and you can begin to step into favor with folks as they learn to trust you. Maybe we'll talk it over but that water could be boiling now. Save an old man a few steps and dip this lancet in the water, if you will please," he said.

Samantha cleaned the pointed tool with its mottled tortoiseshell handle. She wondered how the open half-tube would be used, but would soon know. She was smiling at her good fortune to be helping Doc again after all the time gone by.

"Sam, can we have the basin to catch the blood?" Doc said. Auntie was quick to supply it, carrying it into the room.

"This procedure is easy enough to reduce the quantity of blood in the system," Doc said. "It won't prevent madness, very doubtful, but will release pressure. It makes no difference where we puncture a vein, since blood circulates. Are you confident to press the vein to close it on either side of the small opening when we have drained enough blood?" he asked.

"Yes, Doc, I am," Samantha said.

"I will tap a neck vein not that far from his swollen head-wound," Doc said. He tapped into a vein in the side of the neck with the lancet and blood flowed down the half tube into the basin. It wasn't long before he asked Samantha to use pressure on the vein and the red drainage stopped and the job was done.

"That removed less than one pint, Sam. No use to go overboard. It could require another application in a couple of days if swelling and pressure mounts up again before enough healing of the head occurs," Doc said. "Now we have a waiting game for a few days to see if he survives."

"We can put you up in a bed, Doc," William offered. "No need to travel tonight."

"Much obliged," Doc said. Leroy's bed was empty and available for Doc's comfort. Auntie took up watching the patient while Samantha and the rest of the household were glad to go to sleep.

~~*~~

Isaac had a sense of humor, but no one knew for sure why he was unusually happy this morning. He was good at keeping business to himself for clients, so details were not expected. "When I go on my errands along the Ohio River Road this morning, I will stop to check on Leroy. I can let Mrs. Gray know that

Doc Murphy was found and fetched," Isaac said with a chuckle. "I will give her an update on what was done for her husband."

It was decided around the breakfast table that Doc could stick around for a couple of days to help Samantha do the bloodletting procedure if it were needed again for the patient. "I can't say I mind one bit, Sam," Doc said. "We can get caught up on what each of our lives has contained since Yorktown battle."

"How did you lose that leg, Doc," William asked.

"This was a result of the bullet I took in my leg at Yorktown. Sam, here, found me on the bank of Wormley Creek. It would have been worse if she hadn't found me, maybe fatal. After a few days infection set in, but you folks had gone home. After another week, it turned into gangrene and the lower part was amputated. I gave instructions on the procedure and then drank enough rum from Cornwallis' supplies to help a good bit. You run a risk with infection just like that poor fellow in the other room. No guarantee against it," he said.

"I suppose you made the peg leg that finishes off the bottom half now? Isaac said.

Doc chuckled and nodded his head. "I did become good at whittling, I'll say out of necessity."

"Samantha, maybe you can take your old friend riding in the chaise," William said.

"Yes, I can while Auntie is sitting watch with the patient," Samantha said. And she did. She told him about her horse, Brown, given by George Washington. And about her visit to Mt. Vernon, of her ordeal at the hands of Dr. Goodson, and losing her brother, Jonathan. She told him she made up her mind to practice medicine after she worked with him at Yorktown. They made a pact to connect just after the turn of the new year, and start some house-calls together to assist each other.

"It feels like my great good fortune to have your acquaintance and your help again, Sam," Doc said.

"I am now more confident than ever that I could go out and help people here. I had treated a couple of people when it fell to me like it did with Simon Gray, but with your help, Doc, I will be able to branch out." She said.

"What a team we'll be, Sam," Doc said along with his hearty chuckle.

It would be hard for Samantha to wait.

Chapter 20

Parents Sow Doubt
December 1783

Isaac knew a few things about the Virginia Military District. He and other lawyers could often make money because of knowledge they possessed. He was just as able as any other and had appointments at several homes to impart that particular knowledge along with ideas and strategy on how to use it. It was no problem to lack a formal law office since it was a way of life now in the temporary residences that other agents of law found themselves in, too. He presented his price in the packages to take care of legal paperwork. His reputation was building as clients spread the word that he was an honest man.

The information he had now wouldn't make him any money from the Crow family and friends because he wouldn't charge them for it, and it would make a significant difference for two families. When the time was right, he would relish setting it in motion. He would wait until the way was clear that he should speak. Until then, only his smile would be a sign of his active mind at work.

Two days had passed and another bloodletting procedure had been done successfully by Samantha while under Doc's supervision. "Our patient is improving with the swelling down a small amount, a good sign. He also has a slight bit of alertness I believe, Sam," Doc said. "He needs to be able to take in food to survive. The minute he can sip the fluid he will start to improve more." Not one person corrected Doc Murphy from calling her Sam and she didn't mind.

It was no problem for Isaac to take Doc Murphy home on the third day. "I will stop and pick up Leroy to bring him home on my return trip," Isaac said. "The chopped wood must be plentiful by now and Mrs. Gray's boy will be able to do the easier work to feed the animals and milk the cow." Isaac's upbeat demeanor never faded.

December proved to be as cold as they had heard about. Samantha had lots of time to make mittens for the five children with the tiniest pair for baby Henry. She enjoyed knowing their hands would be warm while they made snowballs. She was especially glad she had the cloak to prevent chill. She went out on short walks but preferred to stay where it was warmer. Before she went inside she made a few snowballs and threw them at Matthew, who was twice as good at hitting her with them. He only used the tomboy version of her name when they were alone and she didn't mind a direct hit when he called her Sam.

"Sam, you are no good at throwing snowballs. Pack them tight and round so they don't fall apart, like this," he said and landed one squarely on her shoulder.

It was true about her non-existent ability with snowballs and she would mostly avoid that playfulness because she had something on her mind. She wondered how long she would have to wait for happiness. She must have been wearing her impatience with her unhappiness on her face. She returned inside.

Mother said, "Samantha, you may be wasting your time waiting for Corporal Sutter since he may never come."

Did Mother mean well again, or was it meant to hurt as much as it did when

Samantha heard it? She wondered if Mother could be right but certainly would not admit to her of any doubt creeping in. The note from Corporal Sutter was nearly worn out from being carried folded in her pocket. Its creases were proof of his affection each time she read it and folded it back. Would he ever come or would Father lose patience, too, and go back to talk of looking for a husband for her again? She had her independence and preferred to keep it, but she did not want to keep her loneliness, which she felt even in the midst of a crowded family.

"Samantha, what makes you think you can keep independence when you marry?" Mother asked.

Why was she always ready to hinder Samantha's reasoning? Was it just that she thought Samantha was wrong and why was Mother so sure she was waiting for someone who would never come? It had created a wedge between them.

"I believe he thought my independence was quite brave when he met me at Yorktown battlefield, Mother. He has not forgotten my involvement to help General Washington at that time. Daniel knew his mind when he wrote me a note, which you know Jonathan gave to me." Samantha said. She tossed her hair behind her with a shake of her head.

"That was written quite some time ago, Samantha, and a lot can happen in that time, which you know nothing about," Mother said.

"I do know something about it, Mother, Please," she said.

Mother was not interested and had finished what she set out to say. Samantha wanted to tell her that the information in the letter from Martha Washington could not be false, but Mother had walked away. She had not been part of the discovery of the stolen and recovered letters. Her mind was closed.

A week had crawled by since Simon Gray had been wounded. He was semi-alert and sipping cider with a few nibbles of nutrition when offered. He slept far more than the short alert moments that Samantha and Auntie tried to seize on as an opportunity to give him fluid.

It was a week in which Isaac often wore a smile and had the people around him wondering what secret he had that was responsible for his mood.

Isaac was ready to make an attempt to negotiate smiles on other faces. "Percy, let's go on a ride to see how the situation is with Mrs.

Gray. Maybe she needs to hire someone to split wood by now. We can find out and maybe Leroy could get a paid job. I have some information that may be helpful to her that I want to talk over with her anyway," Isaac said. He enjoyed making good things happen and it was not long until Christmas. He was hoping to put a plan in motion and see everyone filled with the happiness of the Christmas spirit. He enjoyed thinking that he would be using his knowledge to help create a path to better futures where few resources for it existed now.

"Leroy wouldn't mind working for a little money," Percy said, "but it seems best to just help the woman awhile longer."

"We'll see," Isaac said as they arrived at Mrs. Gray's cabin in the middle of the morning. The scrawny boy was trying to split wood and it was clear that he was not a healthy boy with sufficient strength, which the job required.

"Now that's just pitiful," Percy said. "A man's got to have compassion."

"Hold on. Don't touch that ax just yet. I have some business to conduct and we'll see how it goes if you just hold up. Mind the team if you will and give me a little slack to do some talking," Isaac said. He knocked on the door and a sad girl of about nine-years-old opened it but remained silent. Mrs. Gray stepped into view behind the girl.

"Come in," Mrs. Gray said.

Isaac could see that there was no happiness inside, but he hadn't expected it to be as obvious as it was with sad faces reflecting their mother's anxiety. The misery no doubt stemmed from the absence and injury of the man of the family. Isaac believed it was also desperation for what the future no longer held.

"How are you and the family doing, Mrs. Gray? I brought a bit of good news that Simon is moving slightly and has accepted a small amount of soft food and liquid. It could mean hope for the future," Isaac said.

Mrs. Gray's eyes were brimming with tears and kept her from speaking.

"Looks like you are running low on wood again," he said.

She regained her voice. "We will cut the wood for our needs and I plan to use an ax myself. My son is not well and cannot do much of it. I will soon run out of money if I pay to have it done and we do not expect it done free again. The kindness extended to us by you and your friends was generous. Please let them all know that we are doing just fine on our own," Mrs. Gray said.

Isaac could see that her pride would not allow any more charity. She had made it clear. It played well with what he had in mind.

"You can do better than 'just fine' when you get to Ohio Country and stake a claim with your land warrant. Of course that is after the U.S. Government issues them to former militia and enlisted men," he said.

Mrs. Gray turned toward Isaac. She had no patience with him and no disguise of her scorn. She spoke sharp, cutting straight to the point with her reply, not at all happy to listen to Isaac. "I have no way to get there and a husband who cannot petition for a claim now, Mr. Hogan. If they send the land claim order, a person so damaged as Simon cannot apply," Mrs. Gray said.

"No, he can't, but they will send it since he is alive and qualifies. As his wife, you can help him sign up," Isaac said.

Mrs. Gray looked surprised and hopeful for an instant. But then, "It won't help me since I cannot get there without a husband working to take care of this family and drive a team. I can do neither, Mr. Hogan. I must do something, but that is impossible," she said.

"Listen to what I propose and consider if it works for you to make a way for the future," he said.

"Mr. Hogan, I have no way to pay you for a lawyer's advice. I'm sorry," she said.

"Please hear me out, Mrs. Gray. Land grants are awarded according to the rank of the individual when he mustered out of service. Your husband would have 300 acres if you make sure he claims it. It is waiting for you as his wife to apply for it when the warrants are granted. You can hire help to work and take care of your family now and to drive you and your family to Ohio Country when it opens for Virginia military," he said.

"I have no money to spend," Mrs. Gray said in an undisguised irritated manner.

Isaac heard her irritation against him in her voice but continued on as if she had not cut him off.

"You can pay with the promise of land after you get there. You could offer 50 acres. If the government is slower than predicted getting everything in place, you will pay up to 75 or a 100 acres, but only if the extension runs longer and makes it necessary. You already know Percy and Leroy work well and I believe they can be hired with this deal. I am willing to propose the same deal to them and to draw up legal papers to accomplish the contract so both parties are protected," Isaac said.

Mrs. Gray was staring at him and thinking about it. "It sounds hard, maybe too good to be true. I don't know," she said. Her shoulders slumped as she became skeptical again. "What would you charge for creating the legal papers?" she asked.

"I want ten acres of land with a signed deed for it, to be payable only when we all get to Ohio Country together. You and your children would be in safe company with us. I extend that offer for one week since you need time to think about it," Isaac said. He got up to leave. "I will come back in a week to hear what you have decided. We insist upon splitting enough wood to last for a week so you will not feel pressured." He walked to the door to go out but turned back.

"Another thought, Mrs. Gray. This is not entirely benevolent on my part. I have a friend in Percy and also his family. I do want this for them, too, which will be just as good for them as for you. It won't seem 'just fine' as you say, to do nothing and miss out on a great deal that ensures a way to provide for your children. If you dislike Ohio Country, you can sell all of the

remainder of your property and return south.
You might also consider how you will feel when
you are left behind. More than half of the
camps here will disperse when the population
leaves for Ohio Country." He was done and he
walked out the door.

"Percy, I think we better use that ax
awhile," Isaac said.

"You all right, Mr. Isaac?" Percy said.
"You changed your mind?"

"I hope somebody else changes her mind
but it may take a while to think it through for
one who is in no way used to making decisions.
We might as well help this boy out. We can do
in 30 minutes what it will take him all day to do
if he even had the strength for it," Isaac said.

They took turns with the ax and in half-
an-hour they had a pile of wood chunks to last
awhile. Isaac kept his eyes on the door and it
finally opened.

"Mr. Hogan, may I speak with you?"
Mrs. Gray said. "I have some questions."

Isaac went inside, while Percy continued
with the ax. When Isaac came out, he had
answered questions on what would be done to
help Mrs. Gray. He assured her that he would
talk it through with all parties so no one
doubted their part, obligations, and gains. Now

he was ready to talk to Percy about the deal. Mrs. Gray was in full agreement.

"Percy, I have a deal for you and Leroy both. Are you in the mood to be hired to work now and be paid in land later in Ohio Country?"

Percy's jaw dropped as he took a moment for Isaac's words to set in. "I may if the land is a sure thing. I can listen to your pitch," Percy said.

When Percy heard the entire deal, he said, "Draw those papers up and I will show Mrs. Gray that she will get plenty of work from me and Leroy. One thing though, Leroy and I split the deal even so he gets half the land we earn. He may want to start a family as a free man and this could be his ticket," Percy said.

"It could be the best start for both of you and I will have the papers drafted. You will need to designate someone to read you the entire contract between you and Mrs. Gray. It can't be me because I am drawing it up. Leroy will also need to sign. Then you will both work hard to pull Mrs. Gray through this rough time and get her and her family to Ohio Country. It could take the whole winter and it could take all of next year. You will need to raise a lot of food and hunt for yourselves and the Gray family if we are forced to start next year right here again," Isaac said.

"I worked hard all my life and if the work can insure our future now, we will not shirk from it. The deal...it will be unbreakable if we sign it, right?" Percy said.

"Yes. When you sign a contract it is equally binding on both parties," Isaac said.

Mrs. Gray's son had a broad grin and was carrying wood inside. The wood chunks cut and chopped for his family was his great relief. Mrs. Gray opened the door for her son and her face mirrored him, as if an enormous burden had been lifted. It was an even bigger relief for her with Isaac's proposed deal.

Isaac said, "Mrs. Gray, we will be back in three days with a contract to sign and more wood will be cut." They drove off in a good mood.

Percy was eager to talk with Geneva and Leroy. His good mood was far from contained. "It's like an early Christmas to have this deal. I can't wait to tell it," he said. When they drove up to the gate, Percy hollered, "Geneva!"

Isaac was composed, usually, but this happiness was contagious. He was as jubilant as Percy with the good news and could not contain his smile as he saw something he had never witnessed before.

Percy threw the gate open and picked Geneva up and spun her around. "We will have land when we get to Ohio Country! Leroy will too." Percy said. He whirled Geneva around again and told her the details as they stood in the snow. "Hard work will have a reward this time!" he said.

The evening assembly was happy for the Crow family and all friends gathered around their table. Leroy had questions and Isaac enjoyed answering them and adding to everyone's understanding of the deal he was about to broker.

"What could make this deal fall through?" Leroy asked.

"The only circumstance that could make it null and void is if Simon Gray dies before the government land warrant is in effect. If he dies afterward, it will not alter the land ownership and the contract's validity. The widow would own the land and be able to continue with the deal, in fact, would be compelled to follow through. I have made it just as clear to Mrs. Gray, so that no other surprises can interfere with the success of it," Isaac said.

Percy offered his hand and Isaac was glad to robustly shake the hand of his good friend. Leroy and William shook hands all around as well.

Isaac drew the papers up with Samantha's full knowledge. A technicality existed where she would have to sign papers to give Percy and Leroy permission to hire themselves out under the contract for Mrs. Gray. Samantha would sign as Widow Goodson to allow her slaves to work for other than herself. She was initially chosen to read the contract to Percy, Geneva, and Leroy, but deferred to Father to read it. She hoped it created good will with him.

Isaac did not linger in drawing up the contract. The whole thing was accomplished inside three days from the time he had a contract made up at the Ohio River Road newspaper and office business. All parties had signed. Mrs. Gray and her five children would have a future while Percy and his family would have land when they gained freedom in Ohio Country. Isaac thought it was quite a Christmas present. They all did. Isaac believed that all smiles were permanent for much longer than the Christmas season.

It was time for Christmas decor to be brought and hung on doors and for adornment of fireplace mantles. Samantha was happy to ride into the country to look for ground pine and bittersweet. The day was warmer than some others before it. Brown trotted with a light step. Matthew was her passenger and in a happy mood, since his hunting for small game had shown him where the ground pine was located. The bittersweet grew in some of the same locations as the pine lace. On their return they stopped at Jonathan's grave and circled the gravestone with the lacy pine, also adding several clusters of the orange and red berries of bittersweet twigs. They stood together admiring it and fondly remembering Jonathan. Neither felt shame of the tears shed together.

The decoration of their fireplace mantel left extra ropes of the curly pine and red-orange clusters of berries to be given to the Gray family. The fresh decor would be kept outside in the coolness until they made a trip to visit the family. Matthew helped Samantha pile it into a wooden box in the back of a covered wagon.

Only two days remained before Christmas, and Samantha was ready to go after the snake skin items that she had commissioned the milliner to make. She first thought to go alone or invite Matthew, but Father volunteered to go with her to pick up her goods. It was his first time to ride in a two-wheel chaise. Samantha could see out of the corner of her eyes that Father wore a pleased look at her ability to handle the trap. She heard him clear his throat and it made her wonder if he was about to say something she did not expect. What was wrong?

"Please Pullover to the side of the road, Samantha," he said.

Her heart was beating faster and it didn't go well with the knot that formed in her belly.

"Samantha, you and your mother seem to be at odds again. It is not a good feeling with Christmas so close. What do you think can be done to change that?" he said.

She felt the heat in her cheeks and she knew anger could get the best of her if she were not careful. She was unconsciously twisting her long hair into a ringlet pulled to the side and around the front, biding her time to choose the right words.

"Father, it is hurtful that Mother believes I am wasting my time waiting on a soldier she is convinced will not come. She is trying to cause me to doubt him and I will never do that until I have proof that he is not coming," Samantha said.

"I believe I may bear the blame here, Samantha. Your mother is feeling renewed doubt from something I should not have said until after Christmas. I don't want the joy of the season to be absent from this family when there is so much to be thankful for," he said.

She met his eyes with her straight gaze. "What did you say that caused Mother to have doubt?" she asked. Her eyes did not waver or leave Father's face.

"I mentioned that several soldiers have returned to their families in camps locally and there is a rumor that a peace treaty was signed. Would they be home otherwise?" Father said.

Samantha paused to think. "Would they be home otherwise?" She repeated.

She twisted her hair tight and let go, sinking back in the seat. Her hands were in her lap and she could hardly get her voice under control. She hated the idea that her voice would be shaky and tears would not be far from the surface. She waited another long moment to speak. She wished to speak with conviction.

Samantha's innermost thoughts held dread as she wondered, *why must both parents sow doubt and constantly put me on guard, eroding my own decisions for the future? It is as if a snake is ready with poisonous venom to strike against a soft spot.* She must persevere and keep her hard-won independence.

Samantha sat up straight and turned to look directly at Father.

"I believe General Washington would send as many as possible of his men on leave for the season. Maybe he needs a few of his most trusted men close even if there is a signed treaty and he may have other reasons we know nothing about. I know Corporal Daniel Sutter is one of his most trusted men. I chose not to listen to rumor," Samantha said.

"I apologize for jumping ahead and we can take it up after Christmas, Samantha. Can you be counted upon to be more contrite and pleasant to Mother rather than acting as if she is only to be tolerated?" Father said.

Samantha was not happy, not the least, but it was up to her now and she would give a satisfactory answer to keeping the peace for Christmas. After all, Father had apologized for the short term, too.

Contrite. Of all things...wasn't that a word that Dr. Goodson had used when telling her of his expectations for his new wife? Anger would do her no good now and she could manage compliance for the short term. "I will, Father," she said.

She thought about her independence and was determined not to surrender it to Father. She intended to persevere in a conversation on that order after Christmas.

Chapter 21

Christmas Presents
December 1783

The remainder of the trip to the milliner shop was filled with Brown's steady clop of hooves and the wheels turning. Samantha looked straight ahead. No voice broke the silence for the rest of the ride until they had arrived.

"Father, I do not wish to spoil surprises planned with the gifts I am picking up. Please let me go into the store without you," Samantha said. "I look forward to surprising everyone."

"The milliner shop was your destination, not mine," he said smiling. "I will be happy to wait outside for you, Samantha." He used his most pleasant manner after he had secured her promise and it suited her fine, just fine.

The store proprietor was glad to have the specialty items picked up, but most of all, to receive the rest of the payment on the order. Samantha asked to have the packages wrapped separately in plain gray newsprint, which the shop was generous to provide. She examined each item and was pleased with the quality and also that the skin of the snake she had shot was put to good use. It was her pleasure to write a name on each parcel after it was tied with string. The pleasant interval was concluded and now she must go home and pretend to enjoy the rest of the Christmas season.

Samantha was angry with Mother having managed to ruin the feeling of festivity for her and now Father admitted that he was also doubtful. Mother had more influence than she realized or was it that she knew this was an area where she possessed clout and could use it for the only control available to her? Father hadn't been a mean husband, but he seemed oblivious to Mother needing some independence. He had thought nothing of it when he learned that Mother used the flintlock. It was Mother who worried about it. Did she really want some freedom or was it only that she envied Samantha hers?

Samantha determined that she would paste a smile in place instead of gritting her teeth in silence, but maybe it would have to be both.

Dinner was on the table when they arrived home. Mother and Geneva had laid out the chicken and dumplings with vegetables and vittles, which could not be turned down. Fresh baked loaves along with apple and berry pie sent up an aroma to beckon even the weakest appetite. Pies and bread were cooling on shelves rigged from boards fastened on chunks of wood standing upright. Two higher pieces held the second board to form a double shelf. The shelves were full of the morning's baking. Auntie Geneva was an expert with baked goods in quantity and Mother did not mind the help.

With their meal finished, the men went out to feed animals and on return, each one would bring an armload of wood for the fireplace. It would be stacked neatly to the side.

Dinner and dishes were cleared away when Samantha sprung her sudden idea, while she knew the women had time for it. She kept it to herself that she was trying to sweeten Mother up and keep her word to Father to be cheerful. She remembered again, the beautiful dresses that each of them had brought on their wagons. She took Catherine aside and said she wanted to bring them in, just one each and start to wear them this very day for the Christmas season remaining. She had a lovely one for Mother in navy blue with a pale yellow bodice and lace trim. The second one she had for Mother would go to Grandmother without mention that she had brought them both for Mother. Auntie was able to help carry them in but not so sure she would wear one yet.

Catherine was first to parade her frock in front of them and gracefully accepted compliments. "Come, Geneva, while they all put their new dresses on, I will help you," Catherine said. She had no intentions of letting Geneva decline.

The children played well together while the ladies adorned themselves with the new finery. The five of them formed a half circle with arms linked to admire each other. Mother was nearly giddy with pleasure and Geneva beamed. She was past the hurdle of having an elegant dress to wear. She was wearing it in merry company.

The surprised and pleased glances were appreciated when Isaac, Percy, and William saw the new dresses on their wives. Samantha could not help feeling left out at that moment but was still happy for them. Grandmother's arms went around her and filled her with warmth. She stole a glance at Father whom she could tell was triumphant with the result of his management of her.

A plan was hatched, in Mother's words, to put straw in one of the big wagons for everyone to ride in. Mother was feeling quite generous. They would take apple pie and fresh bread to Mrs. Gray and her children. While they were there, they would sing hymns. It was a spirited gesture to invent fun for the children of both households and wouldn't hurt for adults to enjoy the festive mood. The snow on the ground was a delight to the children. They continued to slip and frolic until required to get in the wagon.

Percy and William were preparing the wagon for a hayride and enjoying their camaraderie. Father poked his head inside to let the adults of the household know that the rigging was ready and they had all better hurry and get in the wagon.

Samantha elected to stay behind. Someone had to stay back and remain on watch over Simon Gray, but only she or Auntie Geneva had the confidence to do the job. She wanted Auntie to enjoy the time with Uncle Percy and the entire group. Even Gram seemed to feel enlivened with her new dress.

Captain Gray would not be taken home in his semi-awake state. It would be a careless act to take a chance on transport and Mrs. Gray surely had enough work with five children to care for. She would be brought soon for a short visit to see him. The patient had no real senses about him and took in only small amounts of food and drink, which was given with care and patience. If he stayed alive, his family would have a future in Ohio Country.

Isaac had been blunt about the situation out of necessity for the family. He checked with Samantha and Geneva often on the importance of remembering it. The head of the Gray family was no longer their leader. Simon Gray was permanently damaged and he would not be home for Christmas.

Samantha handed up one more pie into Auntie's hands at the back of a covered wagon. "Don't forget to help the Gray family decorate with ground pine and bittersweet that Matthew and I gathered for them," she said. "Have a good outing everyone," Samantha called to the wagon-load of family and friends as they pulled away.

She was pleased they were off on a happy jaunt. It was inventive of Mother, perhaps another smidgeon of independence creeping in. Samantha crossed her arms over her chest and raised her eyebrows. Being cold was a convenient disguise for smugness. Samantha uncrossed her arms and walked inside to her small reprieve of solitude. She threw her hair back and complimented herself silently that she was doing well to keep her promise to Father on being more pleasant to Mother. The more she thought of it, she knew she was also happier to see Mother joyful and among friends.

She knew for herself that she intended the same resolve to keep her freedom in the New Year if Father tried to manipulate some of it away from her.

Samantha checked on her silent patient who was the same as every day before. No change significant enough to notice had occurred. She pulled out her journal and wrote to catch up on the past few days, adding that Simon Gray was taking in nourishment. Her mood was lighter and the pages filled with love of family and friends. She would not write of certain displeasures because it was Mother and Grandmother's habit to read her journal. She could only pose a question to its pages on what the future would hold and where she would fit her freedom into the future.

So much uncertainty had been foisted upon her thoughts because her parents meant well. She knew they wanted the best for her, but it was no consolation when her own plans did not agree with them. She wanted to be especially sweet to make the season happy in spite of longing for her real life to start. How long must she wait?

The knuckles on the door were insistent as the knock startled Samantha and her journal slammed shut and fell to the floor. Her hand flew to the flintlock and lingered in the pocket. She drew her hand back, thinking how silly she was to be frightened. There was no reason to believe someone was lying in wait to do her wrong the moment she was finally alone in the house.

Her thoughts came to better sense as she realized she had an unnatural fear lingering from her experience at the merciless hands of Dr. Goodson. She would have no independence at all if she failed to be alone without fear for a few hours. She bent and picked up the journal to replace it on the table.

Maybe Doc Murphy was making a visit. The thought made her warm to a ready smile.

Samantha lifted her chin, wet her lips and took shaky steps toward the door. Her indecision before the hesitant steps gave time for another set of rapping and she jumped. Would it hurt to cock the flintlock in case it was needed? Her thoughts were a struggle as she touched the cold filigree and smoothed down her plumed skirt. She was still brave and independent, she told herself as she forced her out-reached hand to lift the latch and open the door.

"Sam! Samantha...I've found you." Corporal Sutter said.

Her knees buckled, but he caught her as they leaned on each other for support.

"Daniel, at last you've come!" She spoke jubilantly, while loving the sound of her name that had come from his lips.

With an unblinking gaze, they looked into each other's eyes. He picked her up and swung her around with her arms wrapped around his neck. He put her down next to the festive fireplace and knelt on one knee as he reached for her hand.

"Will you marry me, my dearest Samantha?" he asked.

"Yes, my love, after you have asked Father," she answered, "and after my 16th birthday in March."

"I planned to ask him as soon as I was sure you would agree," Daniel said. He kissed the back of her hand and stood to pull her close. Samantha's cheeks deepened as their eyes held devotion for the moments they stood touching. Samantha stepped back from the sweetest embrace she had ever known.

"I have so much I must tell you and so much I want to learn about you while we make our plans," Samantha said. She reached inside her pocket under the velvet plume of her dress and pulled the flintlock into view. "I am glad I decided not to cock my handy gun before opening the door," she said with a laugh.

Daniel laughed with her. "Does this mean that married life with you promises to be exciting and unpredictable?" he said.

The End

Bibliography

Books:

Daniel P. Murphy, Ph. D. *The Everything American Revolution Book.* Avon, Mass.: Adams media, F & W Publications, Inc., 2008.

Norton, Mary Beth. *Liberty's Daughters, The Revolutionary Experience of Women, 1750 - 1800.* Sage House, 512 E. State Street, Ithaca, NY 14850: Cornell University Press, 1996.

Berkin, Carol. *Revolutionary Mothers.* Vintage books of Random House, 2005.

McLaurin, Melton A. Celia, *A Slave (A True Story).* Avon Press, An Imprint of Harper Collins Publishers, 1993 and 1999.

Tanya W. Dean, B.A., History, Whittenberg University and W. David Speas, B. S., Education, Heidelberg College. *Along the Ohio Trail, A short history of Ohio Lands.* Forth paperback edition. Edited by Distinguished Professor of History, Emeritus, The University of Akron Dr. George Knepper. Akron, Ohio, 2003.

Winterer, Carol. *The Mirror of Antiquity, American Women and the Classical Tradition, 1750 - 1900*. Sage house, 512 E. State Street, Ithaca, NY 14850: Cornell University Press, 2007 and 2009.

Online Research:
Wine, "Murder and Thieves", http://hogsheadwine.wordpress.com/. Part 1 - Twelve bottles of wine, the major part of which, they drank. 2013.

The Food Timeline - Colonial American and 17th & 18th Century. n.d. http://www.foodtimeline.org/foodcolonial.html#colonialmealtimes.

Pinterest. n.d. http://www.pinterest.com/danabriggs/old-leather (accessed 2013).

Ancestry.com. Freepages.genealogy.rootsweb.ancestry.com/sunnyann/map-us, map-us 1783 (accessed 2013).

"How Stuff Works." n.d. http://science.howstuffworks.com/flintlock2.htm.

"Ohio Water Sources," n.d. http://ohioline.osu.edu/aex-fact/0480 45.html.

"Wiki Projects Roots Music: banjo origins." n.d.

"Wikipedia, the Free Encyclopedia (Virginia Military)." Virginia Military District. n.d.   http://en,wikipedia.org/wiki/Virginia Military District (accessed 2013).

"Spanish flintlock pistol."   n.d. http://bhappraisals.com (accessed 2013).

"A Brief History of Bloodletting" www.history.com/news/a-brief-history-of-bloodletting, by Jennie Cohen.

Bloodletting – PBS
Early practices – Upstate Medical Student Program, a brief history of bloodletting by Gilbert R. Seigworth, M.D. of Vestal, NY. He is affiliated with Charles Wilson Memorial Hospital of Johnson City, NY, and Ideal Hospital of Endicott, NY. (on-line)

Snake Bite
Wikipedia - revised December 2012: References article by Gurave Akrami; PowerPoint presentation by Dr. Pratheeba Durairaj, M.D., D.A.; pictures by Mayo Clinic staff and Google for display.

Chapter Notes

Chapter 1

1 - Wheelwright; skilled repairman of wagon wheels, rigs, and harnesses, also is a maker of new rigs.

2 - Privies or a privy; are known as out-house, a toilet shack.

3 – Adjourned; suspended (stopped), perhaps to be continue at another date.

Chapter 3

1 – Trailblazer; This is the term for a person who has experience and knowledge of how to get from one point to another, having the experience and is for hire to lead those without that knowledge.

Chapter 6

1 – Trough; a long narrow, generally shallow receptacle. Can be especially for holding water or feed for animals, but not limited to that, a gutter under the eaves of a roof, a depression in land.

Chapter 10

1 - Daniel Boone; He lived from 1734 - 1820 and was 49 during this trailblazing episode. He was number six in a family of Quakers with seven children. He became legendary for marksmanship with his musket, hunting, trapping, and trailblazing. He knew many Indian tribes, including the Shawnee and Iroquois as friend and sometimes foe. His forays into Kentucky land, which was still Virginia's domain in these years, saw him as a Buffalo hunter, trailblazer and a teamster (wagon driver). His skills made him a Captain in the Virginia militia. Legend has laced his life with fact and fiction.

Chapter 14

1 – Farrier; One who shoes horses primarily but may treat them medically, may also include blacksmithing.

2 – Cuspidor; spittoon, a bowl-shaped receptacle, metal vessel for spitting into.

3 – Pounds, Shillings, and Pence; Before the Civil War (1861) inflation went up and down. A gravestone and engraving could cost the equivalent of $3, $7 or $9 dollars depending on inflation from one year to the

next. Pounds, shillings, and pence were still used. A gravestone could be bartered for a half years rent or two month's food (meat and potatoes). Fifteen (15) shillings could buy 10 bushels of potatoes.

One Hundred (100) Pounds; roughly equivalent to $500.00. No hard and fast rule exists for the exact price.

Chapter 15

1 - Chaise; a light open carriage for one or two people.

2 – Trap; means the same as a small buggy or chaise.

3.-.Milliner; A person who makes trims, designs, or sells women's hats, a seller of ribbons, laces, notions and or women's finery, Profession or business of a milliner. (American Heritage Dictionary)

Chapter 16

1 – Northwest Territory Treaty; On slavery; one hundred years later, and after the Civil War, the 13th Amendment to the United States Constitution would repeat words from the NW Ordinance. It ended slavery in the United States.

Chapter 17

1 – Cloak; a cape that closes at the neck and has slits for hand openings (no sleeves) and a hood.

2 - Crevasse or crevice; a deep fissure, a narrow crack, opening or split in the earth.

3 - Moonstruck; Insane, damaged beyond ability to have real sense.

4 - Precipice; very steep cliff or rock-face

Chapter 19

1 - Bloodletting; Bloodletting is one of the humanity's oldest medical practices, dating back thousands of years and linked to many ancient cultures, including the Mayans, Aztecs, Egyptians and Mesopotamians. The typical purpose was to cure a person suffering from some kind of infirmity (leprosy, plague, pneumonia, stroke, inflammation, herpes, acne – pretty much anything). The patient was pierced or cut and then drained of several ounces of blood until they fainted.

Chapter 21

1 – Vittles; seasoning for foods, pickles to enhance a meal, condiments adding flavor, mustards and spices

ABOUT THE AUTHOR

Gail has studied independently in creative writing, literature, and is working with MFA material, with an emphasis on Creative Writing - Fiction through Empire State College. She authored her first novella, *Samantha's Revolution*, (Author House) for young adults in December 2012. Second in the Samantha series is *Samantha's Anguish*, book two, a novel, (Tharsa G Creations). They are followed by *Samantha's Perseverance*, third book in the series. http://www.gailmart.com:Gail's website offers views of her paintings and rock art. She is a member of SCBWI, Society of Children's Book Writers and Illustrators.

The annual Rudolf Mazourek Memorial Scholarship, formed by Gail in 2000, is funded by her art and writing for a student in Auto Body/Mechanics, Alfred State College, NYS.

She studied fine art oil painting with Arden Von Dewitz in Southern California. She paints people, landscapes and all animals and writes a weekly news and local flavor column for Finger Lakes Publications. Gail grew up on a farm in upstate NY with seven siblings. She lives with her husband on 14 acres near Ithaca, New York.

PATRIOT RECOGNITION

Gail Voorheis Mazourek is a member of the Chief Taughannock Chapter of DAR. (Daughters of the American Revolution), founded in 1998 in Trumansburg, NY and has many members in surrounding cities, towns, and villages.

Gail was recording secretary for this DAR group for 6 years. Each qualified member has their own patriot dating back to the American Revolution and is documented in the national archives of NSDAR. Gail's patriot is William Crow, who was present at the deciding battle of the American Revolution at Yorktown, Va. He plays prominently in the Samantha series books.

William Crow first enlisted in the Virginia militia in 1779 and served 3 mos. in Colonel. Nawl's Regiment, Capt. Hopkins Co., 3 mos., another 3 mos. in Colonel Nawl's Regiment, George Baxter's Co. and in 1781 served four months as a Private under Captain Regan's Company at Yorktown. Patriot William Crow received a pension in his 75th year from the Bureau of Pensions, Washington D. C. - O. W. & North Division, J.R.W., pension no. S32196, Pension Roll for Jackson CO, OH, p.135.

Made in the USA
Charleston, SC
30 October 2014